MW01228805

The Hour of Trial

By: Zipporah Anderson

Disclaimer:

This is a work of fiction. All characters, locations, and businesses are purely products of the author's imagination and are fictitious. Any resemblance to actual people, living to dead, or to businesses, places, or events is completely coincidental.

The Hour of Trial

For my sister. I hope they have books in heaven.

For the saints and sinners.

You all inspired me to write this book and to keep going. So, even if you never open the pages and see yourself in the story, thanks for motivating me and pushing me to tell it.

The Hour of Trial

Because you have kept [a] My command to persevere, I also will keep you from the hour of trial which shall come upon the whole world, to test those who dwell on the earth.

-Revelation 3:10

PREFACE

$\mathcal{E}$veryone can think of at least one thing they would say is wrong

with the world. It's broken! The really worrying thing is that it only seems to be getting worse. Human trafficking, drug use, child abuse, murder, robbery, the list goes on and on. But for every problem in the world, there are not many solutions.

This novel was written as a message of hope in a broken world. It presents the solution in an action-packed adventure of seeking the truth. This story is relatable; anyone who picks it up can see themselves in it. These characters represent real people with real issues, and they aren't afraid to ask the hard questions.

This book is a message of faith, hope, and love. And the passion of it is for the forgotten, the lost, and the hurt.

I strongly believe in Jesus Christ, and this book promises healing and light even if you don't follow Him.

I promise that whoever reads this book will be changed. But if you want to find out how, you'll have to see what's inside. It's not called *The* Hour *of Trial* for nothing; time is running out, so don't wait! Get your copy and read the story RIGHT NOW!

TABLE OF CONTENT

PROLOGUE

A gavel pounds into the silence, triggering applause.

"Welcome to The World Alliance!"

After three years of the terror of the Third World War, the leaders of the major world nations have finally come together in council.

"For our first order of business—"

The ambassadors and world leaders all begin to present their case as the most important.

"The food shortages!"

"No, we need rescue efforts for the natural disasters!"

"The numbers of the critically ill are climbing! There should be financial support given to teams for vaccines and medical research."

The calls continue getting louder and louder until you can't hear one petition from the other.

A dangerous religious sect enacted war, which triggered The Third World War that resulted in great tragedy until a leader arose like a phoenix from the ashes.

Each nation has come together and created The World Alliance with one currency, one database, and one General Elect.

Violence is increasing, and panic is rising but with guidance, peace is in sight once again.

"Leaders!" He rises from his seat with his hands high above his head, and silence falls. "There is much to be addressed, but above all, we must eradicate the fungus that is plaguing our recovering community." A charismatic man named Samael Abigor thrives in the praise and admiration on their faces.

"And who is this fungus?" A nasally voice pipes up from the back of the room.

"A group stuck in the past and willing to do anything to stop this new world order. I call them the Adherens…"

Chapter 1

I see her! I'm on 13th street, requesting backup. Over." One officer yells into his mic while pursuing his target.

"Copy that. Stay with her, and we'll circle around. Be careful; these people are dangerous." He hears in response, picking up the pace with burning legs.

This chase has been going on for over an hour. The target seems like she is following an internal map of some kind. Unfortunately, said map has many twists, turns and places to hide. This is typical this close to downtown DC, especially after the bombing here, which makes this place look like something out of a dystopian action and adventure movie.

At least, the White House still stands. It kind of makes you wonder; with many of the surrounding areas, not to mention the rest of the US, in ruins and the White House still stands tall like a desert wildflower untouched by its harsh surroundings.

The target turns quickly left near what's remaining of an apartment building, interrupting the officer's thoughts. Speeding up to not lose her, the officer also makes a left and is greeted by the sight of broken homes and empty streets but no young women.

He takes out his weapon and walks slowly, careful not to step on anything that will give away his position since he is still waiting for backup and doesn't want to be turned into a dummy for target practice. Cautiously, he checks behind all the potential hiding places he sees, weapon at the ready. There is a kill-on-sight order for these radicals. It's a kill-or-be-killed world here, and if it's a decision between eliminating the threats and a peaceful world, well, it is an easy choice.

He continues his search, knowing that his people will be delayed since she didn't stay on course but is unwilling to speak on the comm so close to enemy territory. Turning yet another corner, he hears a gasp before confirming that he's got her.

Looking at her, though, he doesn't see a terrorist, even though he knows that most hide their true identities behind a look of innocence. The tears in her eyes, coily hair—hurriedly styled, from the looks of it, in two space buns— hands raised, and wide dark brown eyes a few shades darker than her rich sepia skin. She looks every part a trustworthy young woman maybe in her twenties.

However, years on the job have taught him not to trust his eyes but his gut. The only problem is that his gut tells him not to shoot this young girl.

"Please. I'm not a terrorist. Please don't... Please don't kill me. Please... I'm just scared. I haven't done anything wrong. Please "

"Stop talking!" The officer states through clenched teeth.

Kill on sight. But the pleading! And she is so young, like his sister before she disappeared. "Why did you run if you're innocent?" He questions.

"I was scared!" She yells, seeing a bit of hope at not being outright killed. "I'm all alone here. I don't want to die, but I don't want to be a prisoner. Don't you see what's happening? They're controlling everything!"

"We're at war; what do you expect?" He responds, feeling grateful that he didn't shoot her but still wary.

"Please." She starts with the pleading once again, making him roll his eyes. "If you take me in, I'll be tortured and killed. If... if you can't let me go then, I guess I, I mean you could— should! You should just ki— "she takes a deep breath and looks him in the eye. "Take me out."

Her voice still quivers, making it clear that she is terrified. There's no way a radical could be this good, right? And aren't they supposed to be fanatical? If she is keen on dying, why hasn't she taken both of them out?

"This isn't right." He mumbles, putting down his gun for the first time since the beginning of the encounter, making her look into his gray eyes in confusion. "Go."

She stares at him for a while longer, then down at his gun, then back to his face again.

"I don't understand."

"Listen, girl," he begins grabbing her arm and lifting her roughly to make her stand and see him eye to eye, "I'm letting you go because something isn't right about all of this, and I'm going to figure it out. It's my job to figure it out."

There have been hundreds of terrorists... people who have been arrested and killed for fanaticism and destructive behaviors. But he never encountered one face-to-face long enough to have a conversation. That's soon to be rectified.

"If I find out that you have hurt one person. Anyone! I will make you wish that I had shot you here and now. Do you understand?" She rapidly nods her head, and he lets her go. "Good, now go."

"Thank you. Umm, What's your name?" He looks at her strangely, a thought in the back of his mind that she'd use it in a ritual to kill him in his sleep or cast a spell.

"My name is Zion. And I just… wanted to thank you." She finishes with a mumble as if afraid that he will change his mind.

He chuckles and then all-out laughs. "My name is Paul. Now leave before I change my mind." He starts, believing and hoping that he made the right decision.

She nods and then runs off. Leaving him to his thoughts. These "radicals" seem to have been, at best, misrepresented and, at worst, framed. Just who are the Adherens?

One week earlier

"I will only say this once, so pay attention." The gruff voice of the Sergeant sounds to the platoon of squad leaders. "This isn't just another little fish so this operation will be *very* closely followed. I hand-picked you all for this mission. I expect no mistakes."

"Yes, sir." The four men chorus.

"Let's get in position." All the squad leaders begin to take their preassigned places. "Paul. A word?"

"Sir?" Paul drawls.

"I need you at your best today. I know you wanted to be done with fieldwork, but we can't afford to lose you with everything going on. And I personally need you to succeed today. No mistakes. No excuses. Nothing is to get in the way of the mission. Is that clear?"

Paul's face becomes a familiar mask. He ensures his gray eyes do not betray the fire he feels down to his fingertips. He slowly reaches into his chest pocket, grabs a stick of gum, and unwraps it methodically before finally taking a bite.

"Yes, sir. I hear you loud and clear." The two make eye contact before Paul takes his leave.

It's not like I have a choice.

"Hawks have a visual."

"Vultures flying high."

"Falcons on the perimeter."

"Ravens ready to engage," Paul says on his Hedylogos (HEDY for short), a communication device named after the Greek god of conversation. "Listen up." He says conversationally to the five men and women that make up his squad. "We make first contact, so keep your eyes open. No one goes home in a body bag. Gabriel, with me, the rest of you pair up."

"Proceed Ravens." Paul hears on his comm. He signals forward to his team and walks through the door. He forgets his personal feelings and takes on the brilliant persona of the Red Raven.

Each team member has a color to differentiate them, and all the special forces are placed in factions according to their strengths after training. The Ravens are versatile, mindful, independent, adaptive, and highly intelligent. Each of them can take missions as a unit or alone. He can't think of any other bird that would better lead an infiltration mission.

Two fingers to the left and right direct his team to different locations. They step lightly, weapons ready, toward the center of the building where they believe their target is.

"I won't be able to communicate with you for long." They hear conversation up ahead. "But I want you to send this Telegraph to as many faithful as possible. Even in death, God can still use me for His glory."

"Should we interrupt?" Gabriel whispers.

Paul places his finger on his mask in a shushing motion. *Rookie,* he thinks.

"I will do what my mother should have." It's a woman's voice distorted. "This is her fault anyway."

"Do not hold this in your heart. Now that The Change is here, our priority must be getting ready."

She hmms noncommittally, "Either way, your time is about up, and Mr. Jameson?"

"Yes?"

"Thank you for everything."

Paul suddenly hears the tell-tale *rat-tat-tat* sounds of gunshots in the vicinity.

"Red Raven entering the nest," Paul states quietly on his comm.

"Let's move." He says to Gabriel. Civilians seem to come out from everywhere. Many appear unarmed, and as far as he can tell, no one is attacking, but you can never be too careful. They run after who they can now see is an average-sized balding man, maybe in his 30s or 40s.

They push over screaming men, women, and children in pursuit of the target. Paul notes all of those they are passing but keeps his eyes on his target.

"Stop!" Gabriel yells, and Paul almost calls him an idiot, but the man does stop running. The younger man looks at Paul for direction, clearly not expecting him to have listened.

Weapons raised; they start to approach him.

"Hands on your head. Slowly." Paul commands.

Open hands begin a slow ascent. "Why am I being detained?" They hear him ask.

"Turn around," Paul says, ignoring the question.

Once he makes his turn, Gabriel gasps. "Jameson De Leon?"

So that's the target?

"The one and only." He sighs and repeats, "why am I being detained?"

Gabe looks at Paul again out of the corner of his eye and whispers, "This is a significant operation for someone like him? He does charity work and has helped in the war effort. I don't understand why— "

"Not the time." Paul interrupts. But he steps forward and takes his helmet off, which he knows has a small camera in it. He sees Gabriel follow his lead as he had hoped that he would. Paul walks up to De León with a small gun in hand. "I have kill on sight orders for you. What have you been up to?" he asks lightly.

He places his hands on his head and looks up at the ceiling. "I believe we are all doing what we feel is right."

Paul casually cocks his gun and looks up at De León. "Well, it looks like your time is running out to do anything."

"What did they tell you about me and my organization?"

Paul remains silent, irked that he knows next to nothing about his target.

"That much, huh?" Jameson chuckles. "I started as a street preacher. You can laugh, but I founded an organization that has been putting a dent in the agenda of our leaders. I mean, look at all of *this* attention."

Paul's mind is racing. There is so much that he has questions about.

"You have to die." He hears himself say. If this is about the leaders, then there is no other option. Whether he agrees with the decision or not.

"But maybe we can take him alive?" Gabriel asks.

"No."

"What if there is a misunderstanding?"

"No," Paul says more firmly. "Go make sure this area is all clear."

As Gabe sulks away, the two men face each other, thinking of the unpleasant near future.

"He seems like a good kid." De León says, breaking the silence.

Paul shrugs, "annoying. Bubbly. Idealistic."

"That probably doesn't last long in your line of work."

"It's time," Paul says instead of responding, offering a piece of gum to Jameson. To which he accepts, amused.

"I do have a last request."

"We don't do that."

"I know. But you aren't like the others. Just don't allow them to give you the *Portentum Change*. It's connected to your nervous system and changes your very DNA. You would never be the same."

"Does that justify you killing and hurting people that you disagree with? Brainwashing people to follow you. Is that what this is?" Paul responds.

"I don't have time to review all this with you but look into my practice."

"This is Blue Hawk. I'm seeing a lot of people coming out of the building. Have we eliminated the target?"

"It's getting hairy in here. No eyes on target, but it's hard to — "

The communication is cut short, and there are sounds of gunfire and a yell.

Paul raises his gun to De Leon's face.

"Looks like it's time to kill me."

"Call off your men. Now!"

"Captain!"

Paul hears Gabriel yell above the sounds of fighting, and though his stance stays the same, he is on the alert.

"It looks like the fire is coming from outside of the building. Be alert, Teams."

Crashes and bangs follow and seem to be occurring on all sides.

I shouldn't have sent him away. He thinks to himself.

Without taking his weapon away, Paul takes control. "Hawks, take up compass 4 points and watch the clock. Falcons secure a 5-yard perimeter. No one gets out. Vultures keep your eyes sharp; no one goes past that wall. Ravens create an inner ring. Sandy Raven, join green and purple. Copy?" There is a round of affirmatives. "The crown is in custody."

"If you get any of my men killed, you'll wish I had only shot you."

"You had doubts. That's why you didn't shoot me. It's why you sent the kid away. Listen to your heart. My 'army' of elderly, children, women, and homeless people don't seem to be threatening your team of birds. Think!"

Paul wants to shout that he is thinking, but his focus is shifted to his men and survival.

He takes the gun and knocks De León out.

"Enough of this."

* * * * * * * * * * *

"I have always believed that a man should not get last words, but looking at an empire falling makes me feel generous." A chilling voice says over a loudspeaker in the basement where a Jameson De León is being held.

Children yell as they are taken from their parents to be adequately educated. And most of the adults will go to FEMA camps.

23

There was no trial.

"You'll never be the same."

Paul thinks over everything that he has seen. No weapons, no soldiers. What are they trying to stop? Who were they harming?

There were no statements taken, no interrogations.

"We are not afraid. Though we suffer for a time, know that joy will come in the morning. And with that, freedom. Thank you for allowing my life to testify. For why else would I face persecution? Father, open their eyes! Let them trust you as a child trusts their parents. Though I may die, I will live. This is only the beginning."

Everyone is silent as Jameson speaks. Not knowing who his passion is aimed toward.

He has no chance to elaborate.

"Kill him." The chill of the voice seems to penetrate bone.

Bam!

But it feels far from over...

Chapter 3

Zion walks down the halls of her job, unable to help but notice

the somber atmosphere at Ross Elementary School. With the new union between Europe, China, The United States, Canada, India, and Russia called The World Alliance, there have been so many changes that she can hardly keep up. But she does. The people who don't manage to keep up end up interrogated, or worse, they disappear.

Zion can't help but think of the people she used to encounter daily. Teachers and parents, even children who have just stopped showing up.

It feels like nowhere is safe anymore.

The children don't know exactly what's going on but even they can sense a change happening. Still, there have been some tough questions in class that no one knows the answer to, let alone a twenty-five-year-old third-grade teacher who has only had this job for a year and a half now.

Once she gets to the end of the hallway, she takes her place in line with the others in Group 4A27, the younger students' teachers. No one speaks to one another except relatives, and even then, the van is silent until you reach your destination. There's no exchanging of information or materials while in transit.

This change started with the war and integration of martial law. But some say it'll get better soon since the war has been settling. To her though, it seems like it's just getting worse. No one knows who to trust or believe.

One of the students who turns and waves to the teachers, quickly rounded up by her parents and taken into their DVT—designated vehicle for transit. Every person in The Alliance has been assigned one and cannot travel further than 10 miles outside of it.

She smiles at the innocence of the child and can't help but wonder if the day is coming soon when she won't see all of their smiling faces again because they disappear... or she does.

She never thought that the war would touch her. But then one of her students disappeared three months ago, and just last week, four children from her class and 17 others were killed in a shooting at a local church. The leaders are calling it a terrorist attack.

But there have been so many that she sometimes wonders if there are more terrorists than ordinary people.

"Group 4A27." She hears in the same monotone as every other day from one of the two guards at the front and back of the line. *It's probably a recording.* She thinks.

They all walk forward and go through the doorway one by one. Zion lifts her left hand and watches as her wristband blinks blue once, like all the others she is with.

For one so small, it has a lot of power.

Every citizen was given a *Vistigeum* wristband during the Great War, which was WWIII.

It connects to all nearby electronics and syncs with its wearer's internal electrical signals. Not only that, but it monitors vitals, hormones, and temperature. It's a waterproof, weatherproof, self-cleaning portable prison. Sure, there is keyless entry everywhere; it can be used as a cell phone and car keys, but it keeps track of everything you do!

Geez, this sounds like an infomercial from hell. Zion chuckles, earning a side eye from Mrs. Mackenzie. Zion gives her a small smile and wonders if she prefers Ms. Martin now since she is recently widowed. She doesn't return the gesture; she only turns away and goes to her DVT to join her 8-year-old son.

As Zion goes to her own DVT, watching her wristband blink again, she thinks of her grandma and wishes she could go home to her.

She sighs; it's really worse.

* * * * * * * * * *

The door opens as Zion sits on the couch, reading through third graders' paragraph attempts.

"You're almost late." She says without looking up.

"Hey," her roommate Adria groans, dropping her bag on the floor and flouncing down next to her best friend since the first year of grade school. "Today was the worst. Please tell me why I signed up to be a nurse again."

"To positively impact people in their most vulnerable state," Zion says distractedly, not looking up. "And I thought yesterday was the worst?"

"Every day is worse than the one before. It's a madhouse. We kill more people than we save these days. These new diseases are mutating faster than we can come up with medicine. And the whole 'no blinking bracelet, no healthcare' thing is getting old. What are we here for if not to help?"

Zion smiles sympathetically. Finally turning to her curvy friend, she is reminded of her journey of self-love and acceptance. Now she oozes confidence and formaldehyde.

"And I've been sanitized 15 times. It's in my pores." Adria continues as Zion turns on the TV. "Can you smell it?" She turns to put her arm in Zion's face, causing her to squeal and push her away.

"Everyone smells it!"

"Are you sure? I can't tell if the sanitizing has sunk in." Zion pushes her away, and she starts to chase after her; both ladies laughing as they run around the couch in circles.

"Stop!"

As if on cue, both of their bracelets turn from red to blue like a police siren or a warning that if it is ignored, there will be consequences.

"This is a mandated message. This is a mandated message. This is a mandated message. This is a mandated message."

Their moment of fun is snatched away, and both women sink onto the couch in front of the screen. They are experienced enough to know that the volume will not turn down, the screen will not turn off, and the blinking bracelet screams if you enter another room.

Blinking bracelet. The two of them should definitely trademark that.

"It is time for all of us to embrace a new era." It's just a voice, but Zion would know it anywhere and dreads ever meeting him face to face. *"Tyranny, violence, hate. These are the things that have led to the death of our loved ones. We have since made peace with our neighboring countries and now lead together as friends. Everyone has the opportunity to join in the unity of The World Alliance. Still, some would stop us from reaching our potential. Working together, we can fix what has been broken. I am honored to inform the people of our community that we are doing away with the* vistigeum *once and for all."*

Zion sits up straighter and hears Adria gasp and clap her hands together.

This is amazing. It'll finally feel like they aren't prisoners anymore.

"To provide the most efficiency, comfort, and safety, we will project the plans for The World Alliance by implementing a biochip for all citizens. The Portentum Change. *Those who object to this are in direct opposition to this New World and will be properly detained. We must work together to smother the spark before it becomes a flame. Take the salt away from the body, and the pressure normalizes. In this case, the salt are people I like to call Adherens. It's a word that means stuck in the past. Refusing to see change as a good thing and destroying forward thinking. Working together, we will fulfill our destiny. We can do anything together."*

His name is Samael Abigor. He is charismatic and a natural-born leader. Or at least that's what Zion used to see. Now, she only sees a power-hungry snake. He is the General Elect of The World Alliance.

The scene that plays next is one that the leaders want no one to forget.

The screen fades to show The General on a podium speaking when a bomb seems to hit him directly. Everyone in that building died. There was a mass funeral, and he was remembered. But then he made a miraculous recovery. The people praised modern medicine and the wonders that are being seen. He claimed that no one would have to die and that he would unify the world.

He accomplished half of that, but with everything he does, an angel of death follows.

The scene cuts to a deranged-looking man fighting three guards, pinning his arms down to his sides and preventing him from falling as he thrashes around wildly.

"They're lying to you! Don't listen to them? The government is trying to deprive you of your own free will! This was all predicted in the Bible, Jesus—"

The camera cuts out and quickly returns to Jackie reporting live from somewhere or another.

"And there you have it, another religious radical who opposes the Alliance and has been aiding the terrorists in these horrible attacks on our nation. I'm Jackie Reaper reporting live, back to you, Heather."

"Thank you, Jackie. There have been another two children who have gone missing in the last 24 hours..." Zion tunes the lady's voice out as she sees Adria take out the medical tape from her bag on the floor and rip four strips, handing Zion two. She takes them with an exasperated look and carefully places them onto her wristwatch over the microphone as Adria does the same.

"Where did you learn that again?"

"Remember Johnathan, the computer engineer?" She wags her eyebrows and smirks.

Zion scrunches her eyebrows and thinks, "You know I don't remember their names. Is that the one that looks like Harry Potter?"

The Honduran beauty laughs and nods her head. "He *was* pretty magical. I can't help but remember him."

I didn't need to know that. Zion thinks.

"There are too many to count. I can't remember everyone."

"The flings don't count! And you know he was different."

"Well, I never liked him."

"So, you *do* remember."

"Was there something you wanted to talk about?" Zion changes the subject.

"I did want to talk to you about something." Adria starts, and Zion nods for her to continue.

"It's getting worse out there, and I've been thinking, maybe we should go and work on a farm somewhere. You know, off the grid." She whispers, feeling the heat from her best friend's thigh at their proximity.

Zion laughs. Man, it feels good to laugh. "We don't know how to farm. And you're saying we should quit our day jobs to learn how to farm in some ambiguous place."

"Well, I would be quitting my night job."

"It'd probably be smelly."

"Smelly. And dirty."

"Let's put the farm plan on hold for now." Zion smiles at her sister. Thinking of how hard all this would be without her dramatics. Speaking of…

Adria throws her head back onto the couch and groans. "You should see them there. Do you know that biological change that he was talking about? They are making it mandatory at the hospitals first for patients and staff. There's no way I'm getting that! And therefore, the farm." Adri states.

"Why straight to the farm? You can be a teacher and work with me." Zion responds.

"Zy, I said that the hospitals are making it mandatory *first*. Within the next couple of months, everyone will have to have one. Do you want a blinking bracelet except in your skin?"

Zion sighs. "Farming, minus the smelly, dirty part, doesn't sound so bad. But I doubt that the farmer gets away unscathed." Zion puts her hands on her head and walks over to a small closet, which the two of them can barely fit in as the program finally ends.

It's best not to have controversial conversations anywhere. You never know who's listening. And this is definitely in dangerous territory.

Once both ladies are in their closet, they simultaneously sit on their left wrist as always, hoping that the reception is worse here without the buffer of the television.

Adria begins in a soft voice, "Do you remember when we would go to your gran's house after school? She would always talk about the world ending and warn us to get right or left. I can't get it out of my head. What if she was right?"

Zion and Adria would often appease her grandmother. She never could believe with one hundred percent certainty the doctrine that her grandma preached. Of course, there's something out there in the great unknown, but who's to say what it is and what it isn't?

Zion gives a politically correct answer at the same volume. "She was an independent." Adria isn't deterred.

"Well, that guy on the news didn't sound like a terrorist; he sounded like some of the people I went to church with as a child. He sounds like Gran. It's just like the weirdos keep saying. We don't have any freedoms anymore! We don't have a right to carry; we're numbered like freaking prisoners. We can't even believe what we want anymore! We didn't get to choose who governs us, and ever since Abigor and The Alliance took over, the world sucks. You heard him tonight: whoever opposes the 'New World' will be properly detained. What does that even mean? And what do the leaders want to do about it? Take away more of our freedoms! Soon, we'll be a world of robots without a thought of our own, heading on a crowded highway to hell."

A heavy silence follows before Zion responds in a very quiet voice. "I understand how you are feeling, but you shouldn't say things like that aloud. Even to me! I was joking about the farm, but maybe... maybe it is time to start making a backup plan. Just in case things do get worse from here. I know this story too, remember? And it does sound very familiar. Let's try to prepare or suck it up and conform."

The two young women look into each other's eyes, trying to read whether or not they are thinking the same thing. Adria, a Hispanic nurse who grew up in foster care, and Zion, a teacher whose last remaining relative passed away the previous year. The two look at each other in resolution and determination, unsure of what tomorrow holds or what the plan is. All they know is to prepare and prepare they shall. But for what?

Chapter 4

Inside, kids! Everyone come back inside now!"

Unlike usual, the children don't respond to the authoritative note in her voice, focusing instead on the scary men with plastic animal masks on their faces and machine guns. The creatures are throwing rocks and bottles that make fires roar around the building.

The children's screams of terror make the scene like something out of a horror movie or a historical telling of the crimes of Hitler. So far, there is only damage done to the building, but Zion knows that that won't last very much longer as rioting tends to gain momentum, feeding on fear like a wildfire feeds on oxygen.

Just as the thought crosses her mind, she sees a child who was in her class last year named Jacob, picked up by one of the assailants in a tiger mask, making her sprint over, unable to stand the thought of anything happening to the kids.

"Do you see what happens?" The criminal says in a manic voice despite the yelling that the boy is doing. "See? Look at the damage that people do when 'terrorists' rule the land!" Jacob begins crying in earnest, not caring one way or another, just wanting to get home to his mother. "Aww, don't cry, little guy. Don't cry. You'll see all the good we do. We have to hit them where it hurts. We can't let them win, little man." He starts trying to pull the child closer to him as if he is going to protect him from the cause of his distress, not knowing or not caring that he *is* the cause. Before Johnathan can get a hernia from his screams, Zion speaks.

"Let him go!" She says as forcefully as she can manage while clenching her teeth, hoping no one can hear them chattering. She reaches for the young boy and keeps eye contact with the masked man. Surprisingly, he listens, and Jacob runs over. He clings to his rescuer while Zion contemplates whether it would be better for the little one to run to someone else besides his 5'3" teacher for safety. *This would be a fine time for a plan B.*

"Why are you doing this!? These are children!"

He laughs somewhat hysterically, "This is the future, right? They need to see and decide for themselves who the real criminals are!"

"You're making that really easy for them, you know." She says through clenched teeth, taking a few slow steps back like an injured animal trying to leave its predator.

"Oh, I'm not a criminal. They are! You hear me!" Zion tightens her grip on the child as he steps closer into her personal space, his forefinger a breath away from her eyes. "I know what you're doing! You can't make me bow! Look at you. So compliant and happy. Look at *my* hands, unshackled, and you're all chained without even knowing it! I've lived free, and I'll die free!"

"You are a fool," she says without thought. "If you think this is the way to effect change, then you're all more delusional than they say."

Suddenly, the man takes another step forward, and Zion shifts so she is completely between him and Little Jake. But she does not run. Slowly, he removes his mask, and she sees his entire face. He's so close that she can see his pupils have dilated, almost making his eyes look black, but she can see a small line of royal blue. He's not what she would imagine a crazy person to look like. Besides being disheveled, he looks clean, and if he replaced the crazed look with a smile, she would even think him to be handsome.

"A fool, you say? I'm enlightened. You go through the motions on a pretense of safety. But if both of our actions cause people to be hurt and killed, you are the more guilty party. Oh yeah, I see in your eyes that you are curious. You may disagree with my methods, but it's still true. The leaders are corrupt. All of us are in danger of losing more than just our lives."

"If you are so righteous, why would you target kids? They have nothing to do with your views of the government."

"Ah, but that's where you're wrong. We scared them, but we didn't screw with their mind. They are still alive. Every one of them. But if they are left in our elite leader's hands, they'll be lost forever, just like you."

His rant seemingly summons the authorities, and ten people march toward him in perfect sync like they are clones of the same person. It's funny because there are no dramatic yells of "freeze" or "put your hands where I can see them." They just march as one toward this man.

He turns from the two civilians and murmurs, "Look into the Expungement Project."

"Who are you?" Zion whispers, creating more space between them. She doesn't know if she is backing away from the man or the guards.

Since there are few other sounds of destruction, Zion assumes the others were gathered already. When they are surrounding him in a perfect circle with a three feet radius, there is silence where the insane man just stares at Jake and Zion with a small smirk on his face before saying in a voice just loud enough for them to hear, "You may remember me as Jesse. I am flawed, but the Lord Himself has come before me. I am not afraid." He looks at Zion, then puts his left hand in the sky.

"I've lived free, and I'll die free." He says as if he is simply stating a fact. The officers take a step forward and he quickly reaches his hand into his pocket, withdrawing a weapon.

All at once, every officer shoots twice; the execution-style is efficient but no less messy. Zion screams and forces Jacob's face against her chest, but not quick enough for him to unsee what he will remember for the rest of his life, however long that may be. An officer turns to them with an ever-present expressionless face like Jango Fett, and the army of clones comes to take over The Republic.

"Back inside."

Before she goes back inside, she sees the weapon Jesse held. A little black book.

He was right about one thing. She is most definitely curious.

Zipporah Anderson

Adria paces the floor in front of the television, showing the last

terror attack that just so happens to be where Zion works.

Who would attack little kids?

The news program said there were some injuries and one casualty, but no names were mentioned, which makes her worry climb since Zion is already an hour late.

The news has moved on to some other tragedy, which is probably another scare tactic to make the general public do what they want. Call her a conspiracy theorist, but Adria feels like everything has been set up like a good poker hand.

Of course, people feel anger and fear when they show videos of big fires and screaming kids. But where were the guards? These days, you can't take a good potty break without the guards checking to make sure you aren't up to something nefarious. But when it actually matters, they all take lunch? No way does she buy it.

And that's why I have to take matters into my own hands.

Zion has always been nice. A rule follower. Adria loves about her— because one of them needs to be sensible— but sometimes she needs someone to stand up to authority who wants people to fit the mold. Adria has never had a problem taking detention or suspension. It was expected of her anyway. Bullies need to be taken down a notch. Or several.

She chuckles, remembering the first time she spoke out of turn on Zion's behalf because she wouldn't read her paper aloud. Who was Mr. Huntington to tell her that she'd never succeed if she didn't do it?

The problem is not only Mr. Huntington now but all of the leaders. Fearmongering to get their way.

Adria sighs as she thinks about how many laws she's preparing to break. *Definitely risking more than an hour of detention.*

She goes over to grab her backpack with all of her essentials, including pepper spray, a pocketknife, duct tape, water, and Chapstick. (because who can live without Chapstick?) There is about 30 minutes before the evening curfew.

Adria inhales and looks down at her *Vistigeum.* Well, no risk, no reward, right? She walks forward, thinking *you'd better be alive.*

She reaches for the doorknob, but the door opens and Zion walks in and drops her things to the floor. "Oh my goodness... you—" She stops herself from running forward and stares into her roommate's blank face instead.

Zion looks like she doesn't have the energy to answer the questions she knows Adria has. Still, she visibly steels herself, knowing there will be no rest until the two talk. She walks over to their closet, forgoing all formalities.

Adria turns up the TV to muffle their talking, somehow knowing that this is a conversation not to be overheard before joining her. Zion moves as if on autopilot. She stares into space as if seeing something that she knows is not there.

Adria starts, "You almost missed curfew. I was starting to worry." There is no need to tell her she was about to break said curfew herself. "I mean, I'm glad that you're okay." She is met with silence. "You are okay, right?" Silence. And the worry is back.

She wordlessly covers both of their bracelets, and the darker skinned girl still doesn't move. "Zion?"

"I'm not okay. I— I believed him. The radical, I *supported* him. I just— I didn't want him to die." Tears spring to her eyes. "There has got to be something wrong with me. He wasn't the crazy, irrational person I was expecting. He was unorthodox and scary but not crazy."

"What are you talking about?" Adria whispers even quieter.

"What happened — I can't explain it, but I was more afraid *when* the guards came, and I didn't think that was possible." Zion sighs and makes eye contact with the Latina.

Adria opens and closes her mouth before deciding what she wants to say. She scoots as close as possible to Zion and tries to be as quiet as she can. "I can't explain everything to you because I don't know it all myself. But you're not the only one asking hard questions. People are confused and scared. But if, hypothetically, someone knew something they shouldn't and came across information they should not have been privy to, it'd be a shame not to take advantage of it, right?"

Zion gets that look on her face, the skeptical one that says that she doesn't want to go along with whatever plan Adria has come up with. But it's their only plan, so Adria just smiles and nods encouragingly.

"I'm waiting for you to tell me that it's too bad that it's all hypothetical," Zion says, leaning her head back against the wall with closed eyes.

"I'm thinking you could do with some relaxation."

****

"Remind me again what we're doing here," Zion asks.

"I decided to sign us up for a yoga class. It's normal to have to de-stress and it's even trendy to wind down in this new age." Adria responds.

"But we've never gone to a yoga class before. I hate yoga."

"I go to yoga classes all the time. And that's why you're so stiff."

Zion pouts, "I'm not stiff."

"Well, after our conversation last night, I decided that yoga would be good for us."

"What does this have to do with——"

"It'll just be relaxing." Adria looks at Zion meaningfully as if to tell her to shut her mouth. She would know that look after so many years of saying the wrong thing at the wrong time. Zion was never interested in the "healthy lies" that Adria employs.

"Here we are."

The most suspicious character that Zion has ever seen looks the two of them over.

"How can I help you today?"

"We were interested in a class with the new instructor. I think his name was John."

The man's eyes widen before he turns his face and grabs two tickets to hand to the ladies. "These are your way in and out of the class, and they will be scored when entering and exiting. Do not lose them." He warns.

"Thanks." Adria grabs Zion's wrist and pulls her down the hall. There are solid black doors that contrast the bright colored walls with silhouettes of people in awkward poses painted on. Zion looks through the glass windows to see men and women in various positions, making her groan. *This is not what I would consider relaxing.*

She opens her mouth to protest once again, and the door to Adria's left opens abruptly.

"What—"

Adria pinches Zion's wrist and raises her eyebrows. Zion flicks the guilty appendage in defense, which makes Adria roll her eyes.

A skinny, tall woman is in the doorway dressed in a nude leotard and green spandex. She holds her hand out, and Zion copies Adria, giving her the stamp card. The woman takes the card and scores it, and Zion holds out her right hand, waiting to have it returned to her, but the woman shakes her head and points to the left hand.

Zion frowns but compiles, switching hands. The woman slides the separated end of the card beneath the *vistegeum* bracelet. She does three folds, making it look like a miniature origami swan before sliding it into a crease on the proximal side that Zion has never seen before. She does the same thing to Adria's.

This is uncomfortable on so many levels, Zion thinks with an incredulous look at a smiling Adria who is fixing her hair and taking deep breaths over and over as if she is preparing for... something.

The tall, skinny lady recaptures Zion's attention as she takes a magnet and what looks like two metal balls on the end with copper wires and places them on both sides of the bracelet right where the paper creases, making just enough space for the cables to go inside.

She nods her head and finally speaks

"We don't have long. Come, follow me."

Zion looks at a smiling Adria, fixing her curly low ponytail and takes one more deep breath. Come to think of it, she is very dressed up in her two-toned leggings and black long-sleeved crop top.

"Okay, what is going on?" Zion asks, feeling underdressed in her plain workout fit.

"We must go. Quickly." She walks down the stairs, which are directly behind her. Adria follows, answering Zion with a shrug and an innocent smile. "We have many rooms here which interfere with the signal that comes from The *Vistigeum*. The adjustment that we give helps with the microphone, but we have been unable to disable the tracking, so we must keep going so as not to be suspicious. But don't worry, we will soon be accomplishing that too."

Zion and Adria follow the skinny woman down two flights of stairs into the basement, which appears to be the antithesis of the upstairs. It is dark and unpainted, with no windows. There are what looks to be labs spaced out throughout the entire space with no door separating them except for three on the outskirts. The two women head towards one of the further doors, but before they get very far, they are given one last message from their guide.

"You have one hour. I will be returning for you within that time frame. Don't dilly-dally. We cannot risk someone becoming suspicious because you want to see your boyfriend."

That takes Zion aback before she notices the woman looking pointedly at Adria before walking away swiftly.

"Are you here to see one of your boyfriends? So, are we not here to do yoga then?"

"The short answer is yes and no."

Zion stops herself from cheering at the no yoga part.

"Adri, where are we?" She whispers. "This looks like the scene in a scary movie before someone dies."

"Depending on who you ask," a new voice answers, "this is a scary movie, and people are dying every day. The question is, who are you in the movie: a hero or a coward?"

The door in front of them is open, and standing before them is a man that Zion recognizes. He has mastered the cute nerd look with his round glasses and dark, messy hair. He could really give Harry Potter a run for his money.

Adria walks forward to hug him, and he laughs as he squeezes her as if he hasn't seen her in a while.

What in the yoga?

"I was starting to wonder if you would ever come back to see me, crazy girl." He murmurs.

"I actually started to go to the yoga classes."

He laughs, nods, and pulls her into the room behind him.

Zion watches them and doesn't take a step. She knows her flirtatious best friend and stopped keeping up with her flings long ago, but she does remember this one.

* * * * * * * * *

"He broke up with me, Zy." Adria has her arms wrapped around her knees.

Zion inhales because Adria is the heartbreaker, not the other way around. "What happened?"

She choked on a sob, "I thought—I tried to give this relationship an honest effort. And he just quit. For nothing!"

"Nothing?"

"He says he is getting into something important and doesn't want me involved. Said it may get dangerous."

* * * * * * * *

Zion wonders if whatever he was getting involved in is still dangerous or now he just doesn't care.

"Zion, come on, we don't have much time." Adria interrupts Zion's musing, and she steps forward across the threshold. The room is in a half octagon with three people facing multiple screens showing encryptions. She hears them murmuring to themselves or maybe to others that's she can't see. It's hard to tell from where she stands. It's like a herd of nerds.

She would laugh at her own corny joke if she wasn't so freaked out. But she figures she should save that for later.

Near the screens, the room is well-lit, but Johnathan leads them to a dark table with a blonde, busty woman holding two weapons in front of her.

The woman looks up curiously at the newcomers. And Johnathan swiftly introduces her as Aoife (ee-fuh) as she lifts her pistol, leaving a large knife on the table before her.

"Hello," Zion hears herself say, interrupting the Nerd Herd's mumbling. She chuckles again at her cleverness, but Aoife doesn't say anything. Instead, she just continues eyeballing them. "Okay..." Zion mumbles, and she hears a snort, making her look around.

She sees a man who looks to be the youngest in the room besides the new ladies. When he makes two eye contact, he nods and then goes back to reading with his eyebrows furrowed, making her wonder what *that* one could be involved in.

"I thought I told you to come this morning," Johnathan says as they walk further into the room.

"You know the scheduling is strict. It was a lot harder to get a morning slot for two." She replies.

"Fine, but we don't have long." He gestures toward two free chairs.

"What exactly is this?" Zion asks while remaining standing.

Jonathan looks at Adria in question.

I'm guessing she was supposed to fill me in.

"We didn't have time or a secure location." She defends herself.

"We have even less time now, so I'll give you the short version. Have a seat." He manages to make the suggestion sound like a command. She sits near Adria but closest to the young man who never looks up from the documents.

"So, you want out before submitting to the change? Smart. Before we know it, everyone will mindlessly wander after their evil Shepard and not even know they're being herded like lambs to the slaughter. The good news is that we can get you out of here before any of that affects you." Adria exhales in relief, and he continues. "Following the trend of the past year, big cities are going to be the first to implement changes. The first thing we will have to do is get you out of town, and then we'll get you connected to our grid system with my people. You two can stay there until we figure out how to get *our* leaders in charge."

Their leaders?

"So, when is all of this supposed to take place?" Adria asks.

"End of the week. So that gives you five days. I'll get you a list of household items you should already have and be prepared to take. As the day gets closer, I'll contact you and give you more information."

"So that's it?" Adria asks.

"Basically."

"Basically?" Zion exclaims. "What exactly are you expecting us to do once we meet your people "off the grid" and then get *new leaders* in office? How do you plan on doing that? Your operation is beneath a yoga facility. Do you even have the manpower to do something like that?"

"You ask many questions for someone who didn't even know why you were here five minutes ago." Johnathan sighs.

"And it seems that you have no answers." She retorts, making his eyebrows frown at her.

"Zion, this is our shot," Adria interjects before he can. "You were at that school yesterday. You saw how bad it's getting."

"Yeah, but I won't leave one dictatorship for another."

"We don't have time for this," Johnathan states irritably. "It's not a dictatorship."

"A good starting point would be to explain what exactly we would have to do?" Adria sighs at Zion's teaching voice, knowing it's condescending unless you are eight.

"I'm not explaining anything! You need *my* help. Not the other way around."

Zion stares at his now standing form silently, finding that sometimes, you learn more from allowing quiet.

"You need manpower for an operation like this." *See? It never fails.* "It's good that you're suspicious. Everyone does have duties, but it's not just an army. It's a collective effort between a group of like-minded people."

He's I probably trying to be one of these new leaders with these political answers.

"We need time to look it over."

"You don't have time, Teacher. We were never meant to have our liberties taken away. I've lived free, and I'll die free."

A beat.

Zion stands abruptly, causing everyone in the room to eyeball her as if she is poised to attack.

"Terrorist! You— it was you at the school... your people— this is crazy! Oh my goodness, what if this is a trap? This is a trap. Adria, we have to go." She grabs Adria's hand.

"What?" Adria shouts but does not pull away, to which Zion is grateful.

"Sir," they turn to one of the Nerd Herd standing and giving a significant look to Johnathan, and he nods in response. She doesn't want to stick around to see what plot they may be trying to enact. She turns toward the doorway to find that it is now manned by a huge man who doesn't look to be in the mood to scooch over and let them out. And he is armed, facing the ladies with a raised eyebrow.

"Now," Johnathan starts speaking. "I think you should do some explaining."

"*You* made those people attack the school."

"Zion, you're talking crazy. Calm down, and let's sit back down." Adria tries to reason.

"We have got to get out of here," Zion says to her through grit teeth.

"No, I want to know what you know," Johnathan says, still standing. Three more people come out of nowhere and surround the table, blocking every exit. "My friends and I are in the mood for a school lesson."

"Well, that sure escalated quickly." A new voice says from behind the ladies. The man who has been reviewing the reports has stood and walks over to the table with tension so thick you wouldn't even need a knife to cut it. "I think the lady is right. We should all calm down and discuss this like civilized adults."

All three of those at the table look at him with varying expressions, but he continues as though ignorant.

"Now, I couldn't help but overhear— with the shouting and all— some accusations of terrorism. We all know you can't make that accusation lightly with our General Elect and The Alliance. So, Ms... Zion, was it? Why don't you explain how you came to think this."

"I don't need any soft ones interfering with—"

"And don't worry. This isn't some prison where you will be interrogated or forced into doing *anything* you don't want to do. Including staying here." He looks at Jonathan meaningfully as if warning him to contradict him.

There is a face-off between the two men at the table before Jonathan takes a seat, followed by Adria and finally Zion. The so far unnamed man decides to remain standing as the three silent men and doorman have not moved and leans against the back wall, obviously paying attention now."

"I work at Ross Elementary School where the attack was, well, it was more like a riot— or actually, a disturbance. Anyway, the perpetrators were ruining things, but I talked to one of them, and he said the same words: 'I've lived free, and I'll die free.' They do violence in the name of freedom. His name was Jessie. He seemed nice but was misguided and persuaded into causing terror to children. Probably with a nice laid-out plan to get away from the thick of things like this one." She slams Jesse's book onto the table.

Nothing he could say would convince Zion that his hands weren't covered in the blood of many other misguided souls along with Jessie.

There is silence, and Johnathan reaches for the book, turning it over in his hands. He opens it and flips through a couple of pages with a frown on his face. Zion knows from when she snooped through it that it's full of encouraging words and phrases. Not something that she would expect from a radical.

"You don't win wars without an army. And sacrifice.".

"So, you just use people?" She responds.

"Whether it's me or not, someone will use you," Jonathan replies. "Might as well make it on your own terms."

It's not the most inviting campaign.

"It sounds to me like the ladies have some thinking to do." The unnamed man states.

"And who are you?" Adria asks him.

He smiles charmingly, "My name is Michael. I'm a friend of— I'm a friend."

That doesn't sound suspicious at all.

"I agree. We can meet again after we've had time to review everything.

"You don't have time."

Woo! Woo! Woo! A siren wails just as he finishes speaking.

"What's going on?" Adria asks, standing and stepping back from the door toward Johnathan.

"I told you; you should have come earlier in the day." He actually sounds regretful.

"Johnathan!" Michael exclaims as there is a flurry of activity. People in the small room place devices into their drives, making the screen flash and blackout. The Nerd Herd are moving as if this is not news to them. The only people who are not moving are

Aoife, Michael, Johnathan, and Adria. Zion is fidgeting, which she considers movement.

"You should be going, *partner*. I think your time is just about up, too." Johnathan directs Michael, reaching down and picking up a small travel duffle bag. He places something in his right ear, and Aoife finally stands as if she was waiting for a cue the entire time.

"There is a right and wrong way of doing things," Michael says over the movement in the unit. He starts moving toward the door that all the Nerd Herd went through.

"That's where you're wrong. There is only successful and unsuccessful." Johnathan responds, following with Aoife on his heels and Zion and Adria in the rear.

There are several sounds of bangs and crashes with yelling in the background, making Zion flinch and duck down as Adria rushes forward to hurry away from the sounds. She reaches for Johnathan's outstretched hand, and he pulls her ahead of him into what looks to be a tunnel hidden in a wall.

Where could they be going? Is this the first step? This was definitely not a surprise to Johnathan and his friends. *I knew it was a trap.*

Zion finds herself standing still in a panic. The noises just outside are getting louder and closer. Why is this happening? Maybe they'd be better off being caught. She wants to scream at the unfairness of it all.

"Hey!" She looks up and sees Michael with an arm full of messy, hastily thrown-together papers. Everyone else has gone ahead. "Maybe now isn't the best time to take in the scenery."

He looks strong, whereas Johnathan has a boyish charm. Michael stands tall, around 6 feet, with a strong jawline, sandy brown wavy hair, and hazel eyes. His skin is tanned like he's had a lot of outdoor living. Despite his frame, he exudes safety, and she wants to trust him.

"I can't—" She interrupts herself, not knowing what she can't do. Can't decide? Can't move? Can't run? All of the above?

"You can." He holds out his hand toward her.

She doesn't move.

"You know, his way isn't the only way. You don't have to lean into your fear. But you've got to have a little faith. Can you do that?"

A loud scream follows a closer crash, and Zion expects him to leave her, but he doesn't move.

How does she know who to trust?

You've got to have a little faith...

"I can do this." She says to herself, stepping forward.

"Well, let's go, darling."

She bristles as she grabs his hand. "Don't call me darling."

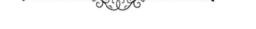

I have been hearing your name a great deal. Some may say that you can complete any mission presented to you."

"Depends on who's asking."

A chuckle passes in the darkness. "*I am* asking, and I am intimately familiar with your goals. You want freedom. To get away from your responsibilities. Your regrets. So much burden on your young shoulders, Paul Fenty. Especially with the disappearance of your sister."

Paul sighs internally and steps forward, head up and face blank as he is trained.

"You see, I have been having problems with a group of renegades who are determined to undermine the precarious peace that we have all sacrificed for."

Just get to the point already, Paul thinks.

"The objective is simple. Find their 'sanctuary' and kill them all. I don't want their ideology spreading."

"Yes, sir," Paul responds, knowing that no other answer is acceptable. No matter how it's phrased, this is not a request.

His leader nods him away, and Paul readies himself to strip away more pieces of himself.

"Oh, and one more thing." He hears stopping mid-stride.

"Sir?"

"Before you and your flock return, I expect you to accept the *Portentum Change*. And if you succeed, I will personally send resources to find her."

Paul does an about-face, thinking the fire in his brindled eyes must be visible in the sight of this blatant puppetry.

"Yes, General. We will not fail."

* * * * * * * * *

"Where are we going?" Zion asks for what seems like the hundredth time.

"Somewhere safe," Michael says.

"Is it in this country? We've been walking for hours."

"You're annoying," Michael says without looking back.

"I hang out with third graders every day. Of course, I am." She retorts, making him chuckle.

The two walk forward another 20 minutes in silence with only Michael's flashlight on his hip for light. Just as Zion opens her mouth for the next round of 'Are we there yet?' Micheal holds up a hand, making her pause.

"Do you see— "

"Shhh!" Michael shushes her quite loudly, in her opinion.

Turning left, he steps forward into a branch, and Zion steps after him. He takes another step before he notices her on his heel and turns around.

"Just wait here." He whispers. "That's what the whole hand-in-the-air thing was for."

"We should have talked about hand signals a mile back." Zion defends.

"Just wait here!" He whisper yells.

Michael walks the rest of the way to the dead end, looking back once to ensure Zion remains in place.

I said I hang out *with children, not that I* am *one.*

He places his hands on the wall and stands back as if he is going to push the concrete back. And nothing happens.

Zion contemplates whether she should help him or keep walking until she finds her own way out.

Micheal grunts moving his hands further out and spreads his fingers back and forth.

"Umm," Zion whispers. "Thank you for helping us get out of here, but I'm going to go. Not that this isn't fun, but I should be finding Adri. She's my sister. Actually, she's my best friend, but we are like sisters. You know, the one with the curly hair? Yeah, we didn't intend to separate, so I should find her since she is with a crazy person. And you look busy anyway. With your wall." She pauses, waiting for a response. "There's probably not enough oxygen down here," *thus pushing against a stone wall,* "so you should be going too. Soon. If you want."

The silence really bothers Zion. Why can't people just nod or wave or something? She needs a conclusion.

She sighs and takes a step to leave.

"Can you just wait there?" Michael grunts out, moving his hands again.

"So, the rambling did nothing to make you respond, but me leaving will?"

"I'm kind of busy."

"It's a stone."

"Take one step back."

Zion raises her hands in the air and steps back to where she was. "This is ridiculous." She mumbles but doesn't leave because she would be more afraid in the tunnels alone.

"Got it!"

There is a click, and the stone swings open like a door.

Michael holds out his hand and steps forward, taking Zions when she doesn't move.

"It's okay for you to move now." He says as he pulls her into what appears to be a drab room with little decoration, a long mirror and two doors. One leads to a clearing surrounded by trees.

"What is this place?"

"It's the bridge. There are others spread throughout the tunnels, but this is the main branch."

"The bridge to where?"

Michael contemplates his answer and shrugs, "That depends on you. We all eventually find ourselves faced with choices. What you choose now will determine where you go."

* * * * * * * * *

"Adria! Adria, are you here?"

"Zion! Oh my gosh, I thought you were caught by the goons or worse." The two hug each other.

"We were—"

"Jonathan—"

The two began talking at the same time and then smile, reminded of happier times.

Zion motions for Adria to speak first.

"Jonathan says that we should move soon. Like tonight."

"Tonight? What happened to five days? It's going to be dark in an hour." Zion says.

"Yeah, I guess with whatever happened today, the timeline is moved up."

"I don't like this..."

"We need to pack. I found the camping backpacks that we never used with all of the pockets. He gave me a list for the road. Here, take it. Mine is basically finished."

Zion takes the list and frowns. "Water, tape, rope, knife, flashlight, waterproof blanket, outdoor gloves..." she trails off, shaking her head at it. "How long does he expect us to be out there?"

"He said something about meeting up with his guys," Adria says, grabbing some supplies from her room and adding them to the bag.

"Adri, this plan sucks. You know that, right?"

Adria bristles and steps from her space, "This plan is all we have right now! The GPS on our V-bracelets pinpoint us to that disturbance today."

"And that disturbance happened because of your boyfriend." Adria opens her mouth to respond, but Zion continues. "What if there was another option? And we could have more time to think about joining Johnathan again."

"What option?"

"When we were separated, Michael gave me another way out. Look at this." Zion pulls out a small pin. Adria sighs and comes to see what she has. "Michael and Johnathan have been collaborating but are in two different groups. One is peaceful, and that's not what we are heading toward if we follow Jonathan's plan."

Adria takes the pin and sees a gold 'A' in script over a red background. It obviously is significant, but she doesn't relent. "Zy..."

"I can show you everything once we get out of here," Zion says, going over the list and grabbing garden gloves from beneath the kitchen cabinet and a thick rope from a tent that was used on one of their beach trips.

"You just met him and are willing to follow him to who knows where?" Adria asks.

"Well, I don't trust Johnny."

"We have to—"

The lights suddenly turn off, making Zion let out a small scream as their eyes adjust to the unexpected darkness.

Times up.

Chapter 7

*W*e have to go. We have to go. We have to go. "We have to go," Zion says aloud, thinking back on her conversation with Michael.

"I need time to think."

"There is no time."

"I need to get in touch with Johnathan," Adria says quietly as she grabs her bag and hands it to Zion, frantically running back and forth, trying to get things. "I don't know if everything is set up, but he said he'd have people just outside of the apartment." She grabs a brush. "He usually contacts *me*," next is a lighter, "but this could be an emergency. What if they found us?"

"Adri, we don't have time to contact anyone," Zion says to Adria as she hands her a rolled towel. "Adria!" She finally pauses her pacing and makes eye contact with Zion. "This is it. We have to go."

She nods and grabs the rope, "We should take the window so we can meet up with the guys."

Zion hesitates, "Michael has a plan that could get us out of here. And we could disconnect the V-bracelets for good. Don't you want to try?"

Adria is already shaking her head before Zion finishes. "We don't know him."

"Well, I don't think we can trust Jonathan."

Chocolate-brown eyes meet honey as they come to an impasse.

Boom, boom, boom!

They hear the sounds of a disturbance happening outside very close to them, making them jump in fright.

Zion motions for Adria to head to the window, and she throws the backpack on and follows.

Adri takes a large 40 ft rope and brings it to the window. She breathes deep, a tell that lets Zion know she is just as anxious if not more than herself. Hence, she grabs her shoulder and nods as if they are not about to commit literal treason. After this, there is no turning back.

"Let's go, sis. We'll do things your way. As long as we're together." Zion ties the rope to the windowsill like a proud girl scout, even with shaking hands, and attaches the rock-climbing clip from college to lower them down.

"Let's just get out of here. I'll go first." Adria chokes out with tears gathering in her eyes.

Zion tries to say something encouraging but hears yelling and voices all around them.

"Have faith, Zion. Nothing is impossible with those who believe." Zion doesn't know why she is thinking so much about her brief time with the mystery of Michael. Their conversation was short, but it was the only thing that calmed her, and it's still working.

"If anything happens, make sure to get away, okay?" Adria chokes out, "even if—"

"Hey," Zion interrupts. "Even if you close your eyes, I'll still be there." Adria smiles, reminded of Zion saying the same thing after one of the most painful days of her life. She was afraid she would be alone, but Zion stayed with her, and they considered each other sisters ever since.

"Even when you don't see me." Adria finishes with a watery smile. She climbs out of the window as if another minute wasted will make her lose her nerve.

Zion looks at the sky and murmurs, "Please let us make it out of here."

* * * * * * * * *

"I wish we had more time to go over everything!" Adria whispers while pulling pieces of her hair out of its quick bun. "Jonathan didn't give me any details, just a very vague direction to go in."

"Probably because he figured that we'd get caught and spill the beans," Zion mutters under her breath and imagines herself as a prisoner, which brings her, once again, to the conversation with Michael, which plays in her mind like a record on repeat.

"Johnathan and I have an agreement. We don't step on each other's toes, but I disagree with his way of doing things."

"So, you think that everyone should just conform?"

"No, of course not. But we fight our battles another way."

"I don't want to be a part of any battles."

"We're always in a fight, darling. You've just got to choose a weapon."

* * * * * * * * *

"Let's try not to worry." Zion reminds herself aloud.

"Right. I'm not worried." Adria responds sarcastically, "Everything is going fine. It's not like we're running for our lives."

Zion looks at Adria skeptically as they walk in a deserted alleyway behind their apartment.

"You know Adri? This is the perfect place for a monster or a zombie to jump out. That would be just the thing to make the apocalypse complete."

Adria covers her hands over her mouth to stifle her startle of laughter. "Not the time, Zion." She loses firmness with her smile.

"Perfect timing, admit it."

"There's nothing here to jump out at us," Adria responds, walking forward.

Nothing here. Zion looks around and sees that she is right. There is absolutely nothing in sight.

"Adri, remember when we moved in and said we would never return here."

"Yeah, because of all the activity and creeps that were always..." She trails off and looks around quickly, only just realizing what Zion had. "Oh my goodness."

Trapped.

"What do we do?"

Adria shakes her head rapidly and holds her hands up. "I really shouldn't be making these decisions."

Zion nods, "You're right, considering the whole fugitive thing."

"Zy!"

"And that we're literally committing treason at this very moment."

"Zion!"

"Sorry!" She shrugs, "It's a defense mechanism."

Adria shakes her head and looks around once again.

"Maybe we can just hide and wait out the searches."

"We'll be sitting ducks if we can't get these bracelets off," Zion responds, sighing. "I'm not going to suggest changing horses in the middle of the stream again, but if you're sure that your guy can help us, let's just get to him in one piece."

"You're right," Adria steels herself, "none of them wear them, so there must be a way to deactivate them." They link hands and step forward closer to the darkness. Now that their eerie feelings have joined the atmosphere, it feels heavy.

Each time they come to the end of a building, they cross into the open quickly and silently. They are so on edge that they will both fall over if a pebble bounces. After several more minutes of silence, they both start to get more apprehensive.

"Adri." Adria jumps and looks accusingly at Zion. "Sorry, but what exactly did he say? Who are we supposed to be looking for?"

"Umm, he didn't say much, just to keep south and that we'd see two teens in an old-fashioned car because big buff men draw attention."

"We're almost out of the alley! And look at us, and we are definitely going to be noticed. I have a really bad feeling about this!"

"I have a bad feeling too, okay. But I trust Jonathan. He thinks of everything, and if he was caught or the plan was changed, he would find a way to let us know. I know you don't like it, but if our only other option is to trust a guy we've met once, I'll take my chances." Adria defends.

"I'm not going to argue with you," Zion concedes, "we're already here, so let's go forward a little more. To the end of the alley, and then we'll figure out our next move." Adria nods and takes the lead, walking to the end of yet another building before looking back at Zion with her lips pressed together.

"Only one more." she mouths to Zion before cautiously walking forward. As she gets to the next building, she sees a car behind a dumpster that looks like a rundown Honda Prelude, which will be hard-pressed to fit one person in it, let alone five.

"That's got to be it!" Adria squeals quietly and looks at Zion, whispering, "I'll go and give them the safe word."

"Adri, wait!"

Adria moves forward excitedly, glad that her nightmare is soon over. Her jog turns into a walk and then little more than a crawl. Adria knows that this was a part of the information she received from Jonathan, and he would not steer her wrong, but she can't help but be nervous. She finally gets close enough to see inside the car and stops. Earlier, the silence was killing her, but now there is no helicopter, no sirens, no cars, no people, nothing; it all seems loud.

Adria turns around slowly to avoid being suspicious and mouths, "It's a trap," just before all hell breaks loose.

Chapter 8

Adria reaches the car just as people come from all corners of the alleyway with flashlights and what she hopes are tasers pointed toward her. She instinctively raises her hands to show herself non-threatening. The men inside the car are pointing weapons at her as well and hiding behind the door like *she's* going to be the one to attack *them*.

Zion gasps and covers her mouth while putting her back on the wall closest to her.

Adria begins backing up but doesn't turn her head again, not knowing if her attackers know whether she is alone or not.

"Don't move!" Shouts one of the armed forces While his counterparts shine lights around the alley looking for others.

"You're under arrest." Adria hears a husky voice laze out. She sees a very calm man of average height and a buzzcut walking towards her. He stops about 10 feet away.

"Have I done anything wrong? This is a bit excessive, isn't it?"

He shrugs his shoulders in response and takes out a stick of gum to offer to her.

"Protocol."

"Why would I take that?"

"I heard that cigarettes are bad for you, so I kicked the habit, and now I'm doing my part for the environment."

"Well, I don't smoke."

"I didn't offer you a cigarette," he shrugs again and puts the sick back into the pack, "but suit yourself."

There's a pause in which he scans the background behind her, which internally freaks her out since she knows Zion is behind her somewhere and most likely not very well hidden. Adria is honestly surprised that they have not found her yet.

"You never answered my question." The man raises an eyebrow as if to urge her on. "What have I done for such a large audience?"

"There was a tip that you and your friend are connected to a group that has plans against the government."

"Oh, so just speculation then? I had no idea that our men in blue, or in your case, black and gray, made such bold moves without any evidence. And speaking of your style choice, the black and gray is throwing off your vibe. I'm not sure it goes with the whole 'chews gum instead of smoke cigarettes' thing you have going on. And your friends have no idea how to treat a lady. No one asked to take my bag or offered to open a door for me. And as for the government thing, I'm not really into politics, so I'm afraid you have the wrong person."

It looks to Adria like the big scary man wants to smile, which would makes him look a lot more handsome for an older guy, but he unfortunately holds it together.

"There is a state of emergency in The Alliance, which you may not have noticed since you 'don't follow politics.' At this time, we have to take every tip seriously. Now come quietly, answer some questions, tell us where your associates are, and you'll be on your way."

Adria mentally sighs in relief that they haven't found Zion yet... and hopefully not Jonathan either even though he is so in the doghouse for this whole mix up.

Outwardly, she smiles innocently. "Associates? I'm afraid I don't know what you mean. I'm actually going to visit my parents since they don't think it's safe here with the 'state of emergency' and all."

"We'll find them either way. Things will go a lot smoother if you cooperate."

"Oh, I invented cooperative," she blinks prettily, "but I really am afraid that you have the wrong person."

The man shrugs his shoulders. "The hard way then." He turns his head and directs one of the men near the car, "Take her to the others." He doesn't take his eyes off of Adria as he continues. Waiting. "The rest of you spread out. Backtrack to the apartment and look for the other girl." He watches her eyes grow in size and raises his eyebrow. He takes a step back to see what she will do.

People always give things away in a panic.

Adria stays still, glancing around frantically as if hoping that a plan will appear to her, but she comes up empty. She's afraid, but if these men were following the kill-on-sight order, they would have killed her already. With that thought in mind, she resigns herself to her fate.

Whatever happens here, she is going to be a prisoner. Or maybe even dead. But not her sister.

As the soldier that was ordered comes to take her to wherever the "others" are, Adria surprises him. She kicks him in his shin, hard enough to make him stumble as he starts to go down. She tries to elbow him on the side of his jaw, but he quickly dodges. Instead of pressing her luck, she kicks the loose asphalt at him, making him shield his eyes. She doesn't expect to get very far once the element of surprise has worn off. And she's only taken one self-defense class in her entire life, so hopefully, this doesn't all get her killed.

"Go! Run now!" Adria starts running perpendicular to Zion's location. "I love you! Go!" Before Adria can get any closer, she's grabbed again by the unfortunate man who was attacked by her and whipped around to find a weapon, which is definitely not a Taser, pointed towards her face. She closes her eyes and hears the footsteps of what seems like 20 men running past her to catch up to Zion, and she hopes she makes it long enough to get to whoever can help her. "Goodbye," Adria whispers into the wind, hoping it will carry her love.

"Stop. Don't shoot her. Take her back to the others." As before, the unphased man looks at her, seemingly puzzled by her actions, but says nothing to her.

"Captain—"

"That's an order. We'll pursue."

* * * * * * * * *

Zion runs suddenly, feeling as if she is a gazelle. But not a graceful gazelle, a gazelle with a broken hip that's carrying a baby elephant.

"Don't shoot!" She hears a male voice vaguely yell about orders behind her as she picks up speed. Adria bought her a few minutes head start, but they quickly found her trail.

Now I'm alone. She thinks with tears in her eyes: her best friend, her sister, is being left to the slaughter. She is ashamed. Ashamed that she left her. That her fear is keeping her from being a hero or a martyr.

Zion shakes her head and runs with her hand to her side, where a stitch is coming. "Don't you dare cry? Not yet."

This is all so overwhelming! But she can meet with Michael if she can get to the tunnels. She just hopes it's not too late.

"Stop!" She hears, which makes her do the opposite. Duh. She would have something intelligent to say if she had more energy to spare, but survival comes first.

"Finally." She says as she comes to a three-way intersection. This is where she and Michael split up just hours ago. The problem is that it all looks different through adrenaline-filled eyes. "Umm, right. I think."

"Over here!" She hears in the distance, and she grimaces. She has got to lose them before she gets to the tunnels. She begins to run forward and smiles a small smile. "This is it." Unfortunately, there is a helicopter closing in on her fast.

Zion comes upon a plot of ruins that was directly affected by one of the first bomb attacks at a community covering ten blocks. It is often shown as an example of why nonconformists shouldn't be trusted.

She moves forward into the ruins but doesn't get far before the lights from above sweep past her location. She gasps and quickly lays against the wall nearest her to hide.

"Come on!" Zion groans. *I could have really done without the helicopter.*

As soon as the coast clears, Zion walks forward a few steps and tries to advance while staying in the shadows. She keeps her eyes peeled for her landmark—

"If you decide to abandon ship and come this way, look for an opening in the shape of the halves of a broken heart," Michael explains.

"Because everyone who passes is heartbroken?" Zion asks, ducking under the passage.

"Until they meet a heart fixer." Michael laughs.

"I don't get it."

Zion isn't sure about a heart fixer but believes her first thought was right. Following this path leads to heartbreak.

She can feel herself beginning to panic and reminds herself to take deep breaths, take her time, and look around. But with the lights and footsteps that seem to be getting closer and closer to her, she definitely isn't experiencing the calm of the first time exploring this area.

After what feels like hours but is actually minutes, she sees the crumbling archway that begins to resemble a broken heart as she gets closer. She climbs in and enters what may have been an auditorium with a cracked ceiling, allowing dust in. She rushes forward to the far-left corner where there is a gathering of seats— or what may have been bleachers at one point— in one area and hurriedly climbs under them just in time.

"I thought I saw her come through here." She hears as a flashlight passes over her location.

"Maybe we should just order a strike and get it over with." Says another.

"You heard the captain, bird brain. He wants her alive."

"Yeah, yeah, yeah."

There is silence for a beat, and Zion tries to quiet her breathing. She can't see them anymore. Is it safe to—

"Enough!" Zion jumps and covers her mouth to prevent any sound from coming out. "Come out, and you get to be with your friend again! We'll make sure the two of you can stay together along with all of your other associates. We just have a few questions."

Yeah right.

She puts her head in her hands and presses firmly against her eyes as tears try to escape. She never thought that her reality would be running from the law. Alone. Afraid. I'm completely confused. It's too late just to give up. They would for sure kill her now. It's always suspicious when you run. Why did she have to run?

Zion takes a deep breath and remembers what made her believe in this crazy plan.

"And inevitably, when this plan fails, what do we do then?"

"That's just the thing. Plans only fail when it's in your power. Even when things look bad, God has something better than you can imagine for you. It doesn't mean that it's easy or what we would call perfect, but you'll always come out a winner."

"Uh God. Help me get out of this. That's all…" nothing changes and she sighs, "This is stupid. Not you, but talking to— What I mean is please. Please, please, *please*. And don't let my friend be dead. Amen."

With 'amen,' she was hoping to get a surge of strength but feels tired and sad. She just hopes this isn't one of those times that God has "something better" planned and lets her get into some crappy situation to teach her something. *As a teacher, I do not approve.*

She takes a deep breath and knows that she can't wait here for much longer. She pauses for another flashlight sweep and then silently slides to the back of the structure. There, she finds what looks to be a sewer opening, but she knows better. Zion grabs the small handles on the bottom right and pulls, and there is a loud scraping sound.

She stops and grimaces, looking around to see if anyone has heard. She doesn't hear any footsteps or yelling, so she grabs the handles on both sides and braces herself, desperately wishing for the few upper body workouts to come in handy now. With a mighty grunt, she quickly pulls back, and the grate lifts up, revealing one of the entrances to the tunnels. The very dark tunnels.

Zion breathes out an exhale filled with stress. She stands the grate with a long stick to her side, and then pulls off her backpack, digging through with urgency. "Flashlight? I thought criminals always had flashlights." Zion murmurs to herself.

"Let's double back." She hears a few yards back and her hands start to shake.

"Calm down, calm down." She tells herself and takes out everything from the bag one by one. *At this point, I'll take a candle or even a lighter.* Zion thinks to herself, unwilling to speak anymore.

"There're too many places to hide here. Call for backup."

"Right."

At that, Zion grabs the backpack from the sides, intending to turn it over, but underneath the front pouch is a flashlight in a black holster. She quickly picks it up and stops herself from squealing.

Maybe there is something to this whole prayer thing after all.

She places everything back into the backpack as quietly as possible, hoping she isn't speaking too soon. She hurries to slide down the hole, flashlight in hand and grabs her backpack to follow, removing the stick so that the grate will blend back into its surroundings.

"In her haste, she forgot to check whether everything had been replaced in her bag. However, her primary focus is finding a place to rest her tired body and soothe her aching heart."

Chapter 9

"This all better not end up with me dying."

Zion fumbles with her flashlight, trying not to drop it in the dark, but finally sheds light on her surroundings to see not much has changed in the few hours since her departure. This is good and bad because that means that the government hasn't found the tunnels yet, but there are no landmarks, no signs, nothing. "And the adventure continues." Zion groans and slumps down onto the ground, head leaning back onto the cool concrete behind her. She is unsure if going away from this entrance is wise since no one knows when she will get to another.

"Adria was right. This is a stupid plan." Zion complains in the emptiness. She never knew she could miss someone's constant nagging and bossiness, but this would be much easier if they were still together. How is she supposed even to find—

"For the record, darling, I think this plan rocks."

"Ah!" There is a fluster of activity as she tries to get up but gets trapped in her backpack strap and falls back onto her bottom.

An outburst of laughter follows instead of the expected sound of rounds emptying, making her take a beat and reach for the flashlight she dropped. She shines it on the culprit and sees a smiling Michael wearing what looks like a thick pair of anti-fog glasses and shoe covers.

"You scared me!" Zion stands to face him properly.

"I gathered." He chuckles, and she looks to see what dropped in her fright.

"How did you sneak up on me? I was on high alert!"

"I picked up on that." He starts sarcastically, "What with you sitting on the floor, eyes closed, flashlight pointing at the wall? Really prepared." Zion deadpans. "As for your second question. You don't think we leave this route unsupervised, do you?"

She stops, "So you knew that I was being hunted and chased down like an *animal,* and you didn't come to help me?"

He shakes his head, "I only knew once you opened the latch. There are motion sensors that let off a little energy when they are triggered. I actually didn't think you were going to commit."

Zion nods, unwilling to share that she didn't have a choice.

The two walk silently until they reach an open doorway about a half mile from the entrance but with many twists and turns.

Once inside, Zion sits on a dark wooden bench and groans loudly. *Finally, Some rest.*

"I need you to look at this. There are some things—What are you doing?"

"Relaxing," Zion responds without moving an inch.

Michael sighs, "I know you've had a long day, but it's just getting started. The tunnels provide some interference, but as long as you wear that *Vistigeum*, we'll always be running. We've got to get it off. Now."

"I can't walk!"

"Standing would help."

"Fine," she moans out. "What is the plan?"

"Are you alone?"

Her face is pained, and she nods.

"I hate to ask, but I needed to know for sure. Here, look this over." He hands her a long, ink-stained paper and grabs her backpack.

"What am I looking at?" Zion asks, confused by the lines and highlighted areas. Even in school, not many papers are still being used as most things have advanced technologically. The sheet looks like it has seen better days. It is yellowed and crinkled; the lettering is worn down.

"It's a map of the tunnels."

"We're leaving?" He agrees. "But the police are swarming out there. I barely got away the first time."

"Don't worry about that." At her look, he amends, "Well, don't worry much. There's always a concern, but you didn't think this was our main hideout, did you?"

"Well... that does make a bit of sense." The bridge is a small room with a large screen and large sitting space. It's not very homey or large.

"The bag is not too bad." Michael says, changing subjects and pulling things out of her pack, "But you don't need all of this stuff, and it will slow you down."

"Hey! That fire starter is important! Why are you leaving the flashlight? The poncho? What if it rains or something? Those are necessities!"

"You'll get them back later. Maybe."

"I'm liking this less and less." Zion crosses her arms over her chest.

Michael repacks her bag minus over half of its contents that he places in a compartment beneath Zion's previously occupied bench.

"You're not out of danger. And I can't promise that you ever will be." Michael starts.

"Then what's the point!"

"Have you ever heard of the *Adherens*?" She shakes her head, and he sighs. "Of course not. What information did you get from John?"

"Nothing! I know absolutely nothing! I don't even know what I'm doing here."

"Well—"

Tik tik tik tik.

He stops when he hears a repeating clicking noise.

"There's no time to explain now. We've got to go."

"What? Where are we going?" Zion can feel her anxiety coming on at the thought of another chase. *Is it ever going to be over?*

Michael takes two much smaller bags and gives her one along with a pair of similar glasses to his, a small clip with an 'A,' and mid-calf high shoe covers that for like skin over her pants and shoes.

"When are we leaving?"

"Now. Let's go."

* * * * * * * * *

They have been quickly walking in what Zion thinks is the opposite direction of where they had come from for about 20 minutes.

"Here we are." Michael breaks the silence.

"Are we leaving the tunnels?" Zion asks, wringing her hands as Michael comes to another grate. "It's freezing down here. How do you not pack a jacket? I had one, but you must have removed it since it's 'non-essential.'"

"Our priority is to get your *visitegeum* off. But when we leave the tunnels, it'll be that much more dangerous."

"Why can't we stay where it is safe?"

Michael steps onto a low rod, and then another to reach the grate and pushes. "Too much activity." He grunts, lifting it up and placing a stick to hold it. "My communication with home, the camera, and your bracelet have already been triggered on multiple monitoring services. Soon, they *will* locate us."

He grabs both sides of the wall and pulls himself up before turning and signaling her to come up.

Zion mirrors him, steps on the two rods, and grabs his hand up and into a small space that looks just big enough to fit them both. Zion flinches as her coily hair gets caught on the ceiling.

Michael reaches over when he sees her struggle to free herself and pulls at it.

"Don't just yank it!" Zion exclaims, thinking of the years of growing her natural hair.

"Do you want to be free or not?" Michael asks, annoyed.

Zion pauses in thought.

"Are you seriously thinking about it?" Michael whispers and pulls her hair loose.

"Ow!" Zion glares at him, and he gestures toward her wrist, making her roll her eyes. *A bit of gentleness would have been nice.*

The glasses he gave her make it so that she can see through the darkness, and the shoe covers fit like socks over her shoes to her calf and make no sound. When they reach the end of the small grate, Michael pushes a tiny lever, making an open slit before them, letting in light... and voices.

"You have already searched my office — unlawfully, may I add — and you have found no evidence of wrongdoing. With as much respect as I can muster, I ask you to leave."

"As martial law has been imposed, we are the law." Zion inhales sharply, and Michael grabs her wrist in warning. That's the same man who has been leading the chase against her. How could he have known that they were coming here? "I have it on good authority that you have been helping Adherens escape the law." He continues.

"I am a scientist, not a vigilante." The voice replies. A woman? Her back is to them, and she has a deep, smooth voice, making

Zion think she could have a successful career as a jazz singer. "And besides—"

"Where is your daughter?" The bad cop replies.

"Which one?"

"The sane one." Another voice adds, belonging to a young, light-skinned black man with a curly high-top fade.

"Neither of my children are insane. I'd appreciate some tact from your men, Capitan."

"Gabe, to the back. Silently." The captain commands, and everyone waits for the order to be fulfilled, and he continues. "You know how young people can be. Like your youngest daughter..."

The woman audibly exhales, obviously hearing the unspoken question. "She ran away. I haven't seen her in months."

Zion hears a hmm, and the captain of the guards begins to walk around the room exploring. Michael's grip on her wrist tightens, and when she looks at him, he is intently focused on the opening, watching the interaction. Now, he is concerned. And that makes Zion concerned.

"You have a lot of books. Hard copies, too. You don't see many of those anymore."

"As I said, I am a scientist. I have always been an avid reader."

Another hmm. "Your daughter 'ran away' around the same time the *Vistigeum* was beginning to be phased into the *Portentum Change*."

She hmmms. "I never gave it much thought."

"Ms. Noble, you've been implicated in a crime." He cuts to the chase. "Treason. Do you have anything to say to that?"

There is a pause, and Ms. Noble begins walking around her room, or maybe it's an office. "There is much to say. Much that you do not know."

"Enlighten me."

"Do you really wish to know? Once you do, there is no unknowing, no matter how much anyone would like."

There is another pause, and Zion assumes he nods his head or something because everyone leaves the room except for the two of them.

"The ones you seek to capture are those who know the truth. There is an agenda that is being accomplished before our eyes. The bioengineered *change* will separate us from The Creator and the truth that keeps us free. The leaders entice the people by saying that everyone will have what they want. You create your own moral code. You are your own God! I am ashamed that I have aided in destroying the world."

"This sounds a lot like religious drivel. The same things that the terrorists are killing in the name of."

"Why else would those who believe in Christ have been targeted above all else?"

"Other religious groups have gotten the same treatment."

"It is intolerant to speak ill of someone's beliefs unless it is Christ-centered."

"Because Christ's teachings have led to increased violence and dis-ease. This war that we are still recovering from started from the teachings of the Bible. And this is not the first Holy War in history. Tragedy keeps repeating itself around this one common thread." Paul exasperates, "there is no reasoning with you people."

"I am not just parroting information. I live for science. This *book* aligns with scientific facts. The leaders are wrong." She states.

"Ms. Noble," Bad Cop sighs, finally showing a crack in his facade. "Why are you telling me this?"

"First answer me this," she questions instead of responding, "Your orders were to kill me without questioning me, weren't they?"

His silence answers.

"Your senses have already told you the truth. Change is dangerous. To everyone."

"This is treason. You will die for these words."

"Though I may die, I will live."

Her words seem to shock him for a moment. "Where did you—"

"To answer your question, I wasn't telling *you*." Zion sees his eyes widen before they scan the room. "Tell my daughter hello, will you?"

Footsteps march around the room in response to a signal from him. Two men grab her and bring her to face the captain.

"If you cooperate, this will go a lot smoother. Where are your accomplices?"

"You will find that trust is imperative to friendship. I do not resist, Captain. You may lead to way."

The two are at an impasse and stare into each other's eye.

"Search the house. The workspace. everything." Bad cop commands and everyone unpauses and moves into action. Several footsteps comb through the room, making Zion jump.

It looks like everyone is passing by their corner until the captain's gray eyes come into view. He has squatted right in front of them and is running his fingers along the border of their hideout. *Is there a lever on the other side?*

She holds her breath as he tilts his head to the side like he knows!

But... he walks away. Back to his prisoner. "Ms. Noble." He says tightly, leading her out. The two of them exit, taking all the guards but one to search another corner of the house.

There is a breath of peace, then another. Suddenly, Michael rolls the barrier open just enough to toss a bead into the office; it blinks once lightly and twice more. Zion worries the lone guard in the room will see.

Michael pushes the latch the rest of the way down, and it opens into what looks like a fireplace.

The guard comes over to investigate just as she knew he would, and he picks up the bead.

"Suspicious activity noted." She hears.

We're doomed.

"Captain? Do you—"

Pew!

Michael shoots a dart at the guard's ankle. And then another at his wrist, which went to remove the offending article.

Michael hurries to exit the fireplace and trips the guard on his way out, making a loud *thunk*.

"Let's go. We have to move quickly."

Zion crawls out of the fireplace into what she now sees as an office in the shape of a half circle. Every wall is filled with books to the ceiling. But her focus is on the unmoving guard. Or rather, his blinking eyes. It's the same one who spoke before, Gabriel.

"Will that kill him?"

"No. He's paralyzed. The sedative will kick in any minute, and he will be out for a while. The paralysis wears off very slowly, but even when he comes to after a couple of hours, he won't be in the chasing mood. Ironically, we can thank the lady of the house's daughter for that, among other things."

Zion sees his eyes stay closed longer with each blink, and she winces, straightening out his limbs and neck. "Sorry."

When she looks up, Michael looks at her strangely, and she just shrugs. He goes to the shelf behind the desk and pulls out several books before returning them.

"What are you looking for?"

He pushes in several books on the same shelf.

"Won't someone come looking for this guy?"

He stokes the spines of three books.

"So, I'm invisible now?"

He taps the top of the shelf, and a light pops on. The light is on the other side of the room and comes on at an angle, shining onto a floorboard in the center of the room.

"She always moves it," Michael says to himself.

"Now he speaks." Zion mumbles.

When the two of them walk over to the floorboard, Zion can see that there are words revealed in the light.

Live the Word

Zion looks at her current partner in crime as he lifts the floorboard and grabs what looks like a small jewelry box. He places it on the floor and takes out gloves from his front chest pocket.

"This is very important. And *can't* get into the leader's hands."

"What is it?"

"They call it Sentience. So far, it's the only way to remove the *Vistigeum* bracelets." He responds and opens the box. It contains a pink-colored, half-dollar-sized substance with a mucous consistency.

"That's... gross," Zion says.

Michael chuckles. "It was developed by one of the smartest people I know... knew. The *vistigeum* responds to biological matter and releases toxins into the body on abrupt removal. This 'gross' substance mimics our biology and tricks it into disconnecting without releasing the toxins and killing the host."

Zion still looks hesitant, and he gestures for her hand. He wraps his gloved hand around her wrist, blocking her shackle.

"Once this is off, there will be many people after us. It lets off a huge burst of energy, so returning to the tunnels won't be safe."

"But how will we escape?" Zion escapes.

"You have the goggles?" She nods. "They will lead you to point C. Then you'll be safe. Safer."

Zion blinks several times. "You make it sound like you're not coming with me." She laughs lightly, but he doesn't join in. "You're... not coming with me?"

He shakes his head. "It's better if I don't. Not until I get rid of this. I'll meet up with you after I draw the guards away. They'll be following this signal." He holds up the bracelet.

"I can't go alone!" Zion shouts, ripping her hand from his grasp. "I-I don't know the equipment. What if there's a malfunction? I barely looked at that map on the bridge. How am I supposed to do this by myself?" She ends in barely a whisper.

"You still don't get it."

"Get what?"

"You're *never* alone."

"I sure feel alone."

Michael sighs and points to the glasses that she has taken to wear like a headband since entering the bright room. "Those glasses aren't just a pretty accessory. Tap them in the B-I-N-G-O pattern and follow the prompts. Do it again to turn them off. If all else fails, step on them."

"You mean if I'm caught," Zion states sarcastically. "On an unknown route, with no help."

"I am no help on my own. You'd understand if you would look up. The Hill is where your help comes from." He holds his hand out for her wrist again.

Zion groans and reaches over. No turning back now.

He places her wrist over the pink blob in the box, and it starts to move toward her. She tries to move away, but he holds her in place until the Sentience covers her wrist. It tightens and tightens, and she lets out a gasp of pain. Her hand is red from the tourniquet, preventing blood flow. And just when she can't take it anymore, it releases and falls back into the box. The *vistigeum* goes with it.

"I— it's over." Zion feels her wrist for the first time in a year

"No," Michael interrupts her, musing. "We're just beginning."

Chapter 10

A flurry of noises erupts from outside the office. But Zion and Michael stay in place.

"I-I don't want to do this. I can't!" Zion tries to explain taking rapid breaths. She didn't sign up for any of this. Why doesn't he understand?

"You can. You have to."

"Please! Don't make me—"

"I don't have time to explain everything to you. Granted, this has been more dramatic than expected. But this is the process."

"But—"

"Put your glasses on. We've got to go. Now." Michael grabs the box and goes over to the downed guard, taking out the darts and his bead. He places those in the box along with his gloves and closes it. "We want to keep their attention away from the tunnels, so we'll take the windows."

"What!"

He quickly goes over to the window on the far left near the edge of the semi-circle. It's just large enough to fit a small human. "There's a ledge to jump out onto. Follow the trail and get to point C. I'll distract them."

Boom!

The lights flicker, and smoke fills the room. Making it impossible to see anything.

"It's an electro-neutralizer." Michael grimaces. "The glasses won't work for 10 minutes."

"What am I supposed to do until then?" Zion panics, stepping back from the ledge and attempting to get back into the room.

"Head northwest until it's back. I wish I could do more, but... you'll be fine." He pauses. "And I'm sorry."

"For Wh—"

He pushes her down, and she barely has time to let out a scream when she hits her back on the ledge.

"I'm going to kill him." She groans, thinking of all the ways that could have gone wrong, even though it wasn't a very far fall.

She hears glass breaking and gunshots ringing in her ears. She forgets her pain and looks up into the window she jumped out of— more like forced out of— and sees it's still intact. And there are no signs of movement that she can see.

Is he dead? She thinks but can't bring herself to say.

She sees something in the window. And she stands to get a closer look, thinking it may be a face. Could it be Michael? She is unsure but decides to go. She turns and jumps onto the road, looking for a landmark to point her to her next goal. She takes deep breaths. Head Northwest.

* * * * * * * * *

Elsewhere

"We have several new persons in custody soon to be taken to the camps."

"Good, good. Question them all. I want the Adherens found." The face of Samael Abigor comes over the screen just after his chilling voice.

"Are they truly dangerous?" Paul asks.

117

Samael hmms in thought. "You do not need to worry for your life or the lives of your men. But this sect of outliers poses the greatest threat to the predestined future. They are called as they are, stuck in the past. They are poisonous! And I need not remind you that it is your responsibility to snuff them out."

"I know my orders." Paul pauses before adding, "There was one girl who escaped. Noble may have sent a message through her."

The temperature of the room drops.

"Find her! I have worked too hard to allow all of it to be for naught!"

"Of course, General. But there is a violent sect that we have most of our resources directed towards."

"No. Redirect and find the religious sector; the others pose no threat to my plans." Abigor waves away Paul's concerns, which makes him frown before schooling his features.

"Our priority has always been to the people. To the truth."

The projected image of Samael flickers, and he stands from his chair, which resembles a throne, to stalk the room as a lion seeking to devour his prey.

"The people are threatened by heretical thought." He says condescendingly. "If we allow their minds to be brainwashed. Everything will have been for nothing. I will not lose!"

Paul was trained to read people, and something isn't adding up. His fingers twitch for a stick of gum, but he holds still and silent as the General Elect takes a breath.

"I want the girl found. And her conspirators."

Paul nods and turns, preparing for his tasks. Mentally, he adds several more things to his to-do list, including finding out the truth and this rogue woman.

* * * * * * * * *

"Captain, I have movement in the northeast corner. Heading to you."

Paul blinks as he is brought back to the present. He stalks forward with his objective in mind and nothing else.

"Everyone converge on the area and hold until I give the go-ahead. Understood?"

There is a symphony of yes sirs and then silence. Many fear the silence but not Paul because though it is often a sign of an incoming storm, it is a time of preparation.

"Incoming captain." He hears on his earpiece, and he holds back a sigh. The leader saw fit to assign extra personnel. He knows that this is a test for him, and the people he is leading are his primary evaluators. They each wear a similar mask and use a voice modulator to give the impression of being one mind and being. They are called shadow guards.

The sound of quick steps confirm that someone is approaching, and he leans into the wall and waits.

The girl from before jogs into an open area, looking back and forth as if trying to decide her next course. She continues for a few seconds, and Paul's brow furrows because she is approaching an obvious dead end. He quietly walks behind her, careful not to bring attention to himself.

"Oh no." He hears her say. "No, no, no, no, no! This can't be right. How am I supposed to..." She trails off, looking around the blockage, which holds a sign of a library. After looking around, she growls in frustration as she sees what his professional eyes have already seen. What was once the library is run down and barely habitable. A large crack runs down the middle of the building, opening to the unknown.

It's a death trap.

She pushes up the glasses on her face, turns around, and squeaks in surprise.

Her eyes grow big, and she takes a step back.

"Hello again." He drawls. "You've had a pretty busy couple of days. Conspiring with not one but two unlawful groups."

She opens and closes her mouth several times, confirming to Paul that she has information on the villains who have been fighting and killing people, including his men and the Adherens. She may be the key that has been missing to locating both groups.

"You're surrounded. Surrender quietly." Paul commands calmly, and men and women start to come out, covering all escape routes and exits. He pushes his HEDY, "Our objective is to capture. No one shoots without my direct command."

"I want you to know…." The woman starts off and then trails off as if unsure if she should continue.

"Know what?"

"I'm not a criminal." She says in a voice so tiny that Paul barely hears her. "My friends and I are innocent! Why is it a crime to want to live your life and do what you feel is right!" She finishes with a yell.

Paul gestures with his first two fingers, and the men start forward, stepping as one as if they share a brain. It makes him miss his men and their individual quirks. Gabriel was the only one of his choosing that he brought, and he is out of commission.

"You can explain yourself on the way."

There is a look that Paul has seen during his time as a squad leader. Always before a suspect or target commits to something. Usually, self-harm or reckless behavior, and the woman before him has that look now, changing his leisurely attitude to an urgent one.

"Grab her now!" He yells to his men both on the HEDY and out loud.

"I am not alone!" She yells, and everyone stops and looks around for the backup, except for Paul. He sees her face set in determination as she turns toward the death trap of a building. Just as the men's attention returns to her, she slides into the lone crack of the building.

Even in the face of yet another loss, he hears echoes in his head.

I am not alone!

Chapter 11

$\mathcal{L}$ion quickly seeks shelter as she hears multiple shots ring outside the building.

"I said alive!" She hears someone —maybe the gum guy—say.

Alive?

Alive! She doesn't know how, but somehow, she made it out of yet another impossible situation alive!

She hears more yelling and an order to cover every part of the building, and there is definitely a plan to send people in after her. She's got to move. She pulls her glasses down, and they grant her the ability to see in the darkness but seem to be malfunctioning in the building. It is reading a road *through* the wall.

After running in what she thinks is northwest for 10 minutes, the goggles sprang to life, leading her to a dead end and now through a wall.

She turns in a full circle and screams.

There is a fat gray rat as big as a gallon of milk whose beady yellow eyes stare back at her. She grabs her bag and slowly backs away to another corner.

"I hate rodents." She shivers in disgust

She covers wall to wall with no other entrance besides the one she initially used. There is much debris, including pages of lost books and what could be parts of the ceiling littering the ground.

Zion sits on a piece of what might have been a table and digs through her bag. *There's got to be a wall buster to go with the footstep- silencer and the X-ray vision glasses.*

Unsurprisingly, there is nothing helpful in the bag because Michael— who she really hopes is alive— took out everything useful. She goes to close it, and it catches on to something. When she looks to see what it is, there is a small tag with writing on it.

Fear not, for I am with you; Be not dismayed, for I am your God. I will strengthen you, yes, I will help you, I will uphold you with My righteous right hand. (Isaiah 41:10, NKJV)

So... he took out the fire starter and left a fortune cookie message! She finally snaps. Everything is just... too much.

"Well, God!" She starts, wondering if anyone can hear her. "I have some concerns about this 'help'. Why does it have to be so hard? Where are you? 'I will be with you?' I'd love to see it! I'm ready, God. Anytime would be great!"

She pants, finally having let off some steam. "I knew You wouldn't—"

Boom!

Before she could continue her frustrated rant, the building trembles, and the opening she slid inside closes, making her scream. Dust and debris are falling on all sides, and the ground shakes for what seems like minutes but is most likely only seconds.

"I'm sorry, I'm sorry, I'm sorry, I'm sorry." Zion hears herself saying repeatedly, crouched down so that her head is between her knees, and her hands are over it.

Another blast follows seconds after the first. Any second, she knows that this building is coming down on her and the rat.

I know now is probably not the best time to ask, but I need a way out. Please, God. If you're there...

Zion coughs multiple times to clear her lungs of the offending dust and opens her eyes to assess her new situation. She glances at where she was when she saw the rat, and her jaw drops. It is completely covered in debris, where she is miraculously minimally affected, but when she scans the rest of the remains, she smiles.

There is an opening as big as a fireplace with light shining through it.

A way out.

* * * * * * * * * *

Zion peaks from the opening and sees men pacing the area and others speaking, including the captain.

Does he ever go away?

Thankfully, the glasses are working correctly, but she has to go through the guards. It only looks to be three.

Zion stays put, calculating the risks of just following the prompts of her glasses. Even though it sent her to a dead end, what other choice does she have?

She crawls out of the small hole and inches forward. She'll be home free if she can just get around the first corner. She steps forward, grateful for the silencers that muffle the sound that her steps would make.

Unfortunately, it doesn't stabilize you. Zion trips forward just as she reaches the corner. That's one of the improvements she'll suggest if she makes it out of here.

"Hey," she says when eyes turn to her. "I was— Aah!"

All three men race toward her, and she runs with everything left in her, which is not much. It has been over an hour since she and Adria left the apartment.

Zion wants to yell in frustration when the men catch on to her trail. She is following the prompts by the glasses to the best of her ability, but she has already missed a turn, and she is sure there was another one.

This reminds her of the hurdles she used to jump in college. *Definitely less clean,* she thinks.

She turns again; a bike turned to the right seems like a sign. She follows it. The light on her glasses blinks to the left, so she quickly turns again to face another wall of debris.

"Come on!"

She climbs over a car door and pushes pieces of cardboard away, and her glasses blink left, so she turns into what looks like the remains of an apartment building.

She knows she is getting close, but she is so tired. Adrenaline can only get you so far. After she goes into the abandoned building, she looks around and quickly goes forward.

She needs a break. She thinks that the guards split up because she only heard one set of footsteps behind her. When she gets to an opening that she can hide, she slides in, crouches down, and waits.

No one notices how loud everything is until you want quiet. Zion tries to catch her breath as silently as possible, but it sounds to her like she is huffing, so she places her hands over her mouth and nose. She swears she can hear herself blinking!

Zion hopes for a scene like one out of movies where the victim hides, and the one chasing them runs right past their hiding place without ever knowing where they went. She's made it this far on outrageous coincidences. What's one more? If she can get just one more miracle, she will be content.

But that's the thing about miracles: you always need just one more.

Zion gasps as she sees a gun pointing toward her head, and she holds her hands up, hoping he can see her innocence in her stance. And try as she might, and she does try, she feels tears start to fall down her face.

"I'm not a terrorist." She starts to plead and knows he doesn't care but wants to tell someone how she feels!

"Stop talking!" He yells, and his eyes don't change. He doesn't care. No one does. Adria is gone. Who knows where her sister is? There is no one left. "Why did you run if you are innocent?"

"I was scared!" She is so angry. Wouldn't he have done the same if he were in her situation? "I'm all alone here. I don't want to die, but I don't want to be a prisoner. Don't you see what's happening? They're controlling everything!"

The state of emergency, the *Change*, the one world leader, the famines, the droughts, the wars. Everything!

"We're at war; what do you expect?"

"Please." She states again, but this time, she feels defeated. "If you take me in, I'll be tortured and killed. If… if you can't let me go then, I guess I, I mean you could — should! You should just ki—" She takes a deep breath and accepts what needs to happen. "Take me out." Her voice wavers, but her conviction does not. She would rather die, and she hopes that he can see that.

"This isn't right." He puts the gun down, which makes her confused.

This is the longest night of my life.

"Go."

Why would he just let her go? They have been chasing her all night!

"I don't understand."

"Listen, girl," he grabs her upper arm and hauls her up. "I'm letting you go because something isn't right about all of this, and I'm going to figure it out. There have been hundreds of terrorists... people who have been arrested and killed for fanaticism and destructive behaviors if I find out that you have hurt one person. Anyone! I will make you wish I had shot you here and now."

I thought you were *going to shoot me here and now.*

"Do you understand?" She rapidly nods her head even though she doesn't really, and he lets her go. "Good, now go."

Zion cannot believe her luck. Her mouth hangs open, and she goes to grab her bag. This man. She can never thank him enough. She can never make it up to him.

"Thank you. What's your name?" He won't know what he has done for her, but she can do something for him. "My name is Zion. And I just wanted thank you." She finishes.

He chuckles and then all-out laughs. "My name is Paul." *He looks like a Paul.* "Now leave before I change my mind." She smiles, never wiping her face of the tears since they are being replaced as quickly as they fall.

She wants to sob. She wants to scream. She wants to rest. But instead, she nods and begins to jog off.

She stops a little bit away and turns back to see him looking at his gun, and she whispers a small "thank you, Paul."

* * * * * * * * * *

Footsteps echo down a hallway, and people move out of the way of the figure stalking toward his target. He stops in front of a door and meets the eyes of one of his men.

"Sir." the uniformed man states.

"Relax," Paul states, walking forward to put his hand on the handle, "I just have someone to talk to." Paul walks inside the room to see a girl who lifts her head from her folded arms on the table.

"I have to say, the hospitality here hasn't been all that great," she says as she meets his eyes.

"Maybe we can discuss that after you answer a few questions," Paul states as he sits opposite her. "Adria, wasn't it?"

Chapter 12

Zion yells as the lights in her glasses start to blink bright bursts in an epileptic's nightmare.

"Well, that's subtle." She takes off her glasses with as much sarcasm as she can muster.

Once her eyesight returns to normal, she looks at her surroundings. It looks like a clearing with felled buildings and large maple trees. There is still debris, but it's an obvious opening. The grass is green and soft, and an early morning fog covers the air.

It's kind of beautiful. Zion admires the beauty in the destruction. She rubs her eyes as sleep tries to overtake her. After the night she had, this area makes her want just to rest. She walks over to a tree and sits against it to wait. She closes her eyes for a moment to give them a break and...

...

"Hey!"

Zion jolts awake and reaches for her bag but finds it no longer near her. She shakes her head to get rid of the sleep daze.

When did I fall asleep?

The morning fog has cleared, so it's obviously been a while.

"Is anyone there?" She asks.

"Who sent you?"

"Wait! Don't shoot me!" Zion holds her hands up and closes her eyes as weapons are pointed toward her for the second time in so many hours. She opens one eye and sees a handmade crossbow, colored dark brown, and a handgun, most likely an old-fashioned Glock of some type.

She doesn't have time to consider the question or these strange people who apparently ask questions later.

"So, what's a little thing like you doing out here out here all alone?" The woman on the right asks, clicking her gun. She is an Asian of average height and deadly beauty. She doesn't wear a face covering like her partner, holding the crossbow, who looks Middle Eastern.

"I was sent here. By someone in your group. Team! Uh, faction? Whatever you're calling your— uh, troop." Zion rambles.

"This ain't Girl Scouts princess. You're at the wrong treehouse."

Zion scowls at the remark. This is not the day for this. The woman smiles a frightening thing in response, obviously enjoying her anger.

"I have proof. How else would I have stumbled on your 'treehouse.'" Zion mocks even though she knows that she shouldn't since she's the one who needs help here. She is going to blame it on delirium.

"Well, well, she bites after all. I would hate to have more useless bodies around these parts." If only she had a toothpick and a country accent; she'd be your resident cowgirl. She is even wearing a straw hat, which Zion assumes is to keep away the nonexistent sunlight.

Zion fights her eyes' desire to roll and instead slides them over to the silent partner, who has been standing back throughout the entire exchange.

That's the dangerous one Zion decides. While the little lady has been moving all around, waving her weapon around with every word, he has yet to move his weapon from her face. She has no idea where he stands, and she starts to feel her heartbeat in her ears.

Any wrong answer or even bad move, and she knows from where her trouble will come.

"Well, let's see this 'proof' then." The cowgirl states loudly, pointing her gun aggressively in Zion's face, unwilling to not be the center of attention. As if she could forget she is there.

Zion reaches her hand out but freezes, hearing a click. She immediately puts her hands back up.

"Why!?"

"Not so fast, little girl."

Zion wants to rip the smirk off of her face and shove it down her throat. *This is why children should not play with weapons.*

"I *was* going slowly." Zion mumbles, but she does move with more care, extending her hand out. "I need my bag."

The cowgirl points behind the tree that Zion was leaning against. She turns to look, and her bag is there, just out of reach. She goes inside of it, sure not to make any sudden movements.

Now, what can be used as proof? Zion shifts around the bag's contents, hoping she looks sure of herself. She casually grabs the glasses and lays them out of the bag, hoping for a reaction.

And... nothing. Okay, she takes out a small notebook, to which they still say nothing. The clip with an A has the same response. A really thick straw? Nothing. She takes out the last thing, gloves, and lays them on the floor with everything from the bag. And they still say nothing. Even the chatty cowgirl has been silent!

"Okay..." Zion starts unsure. "The proof is actually not here. Yet! Not here yet. It is in the form of a very annoying male who vouches. Well... he will vouch when he gets here."

"The pin." The silent man finally speaks, confusing Zion.

Pen? She doesn't want to get on his bad side, and with the bottom half of his face covered and his hood forward, it's hard to say how he actually feels. She looks at the items on the floor and then back at the pair hopelessly.

The cowgirl rolls her eyes and grabs the A clip, roughly shoving it into Zion's hand. "Give him the pin."

"Why couldn't you just—"

"Just do it!" she exclaims impatiently.

I foresee some problems here. She stares the cowgirl in her eyes as she holds the pin. "How do I know you all are who you say you are?"

"Ha!" *Is everything she says so loud?* "I hate to break it to you, but we haven't *said* we're anything."

True. The ball is in their court.

She slowly hands the silent one the pin, and he lowers his weapon— finally— to take it.

"Ow!" Zion pulls her finger back and puts it in her mouth, then she spits it out because her hands are so dirty. "You poked me!"

Click

The three of them look at the now open pin. And it looks like the broody one is reading it.

He sighs. "Another life."

What?

"Who are you people anyway? You're not going to torture me for information, are you? I— I mean, you were supposed to save me from the craziness." The cowgirl full-out laughs, "Am I wrong?"

"No." The Cowgirl says, "But—"

"We can't save you." The guy interrupts. "We can't save anyone, and we don't help people escape reality. There's no genie, and we aren't a group of renegades figuring out how to answer

139

prayers or dreams. In fact, this is the reality that you have to face. It is what nightmares are made of. Some may consider us the resistance, but more resistance means more pressure."

****

"Welcome to The Hill. The home of the *Adherens.*"

After being led though a cluster of trees, the broody guy, who she has learned goes by Ravi, pulls bark from one of the trees, which causes them to open like a flower blooming. It reveals a board that they stepped onto which descends into an underground hideout.

Zion steps from the elevator contraption once it stops into a chamber lit by candles and slits in the ceiling letting in natural light.

The cowgirl— "Call me Chaz" — chuckles as Zion tenses looking around and Ravi looks over but says nothing.

The shutters in the ceiling make the room less daunting. Vines, herbs, and plants surround the chamber like a wild garden. Four tunnels take the spaces on a compass. Or at least that's what it looks like to her. The birds she hears chirping sound distant, but it looks like the greenery follows the walls of each tunnel.

"It's beautiful." Zion breathes.

"Thank you." Zion turns to face the deeper feminine voice that she doesn't recognize.

A woman, maybe twice her age, walks into her view. Her copper skin would not betray her age if she did not have a few gray strands of thick, straight hair. Her brown eyes meet Zion's, and she seems to read her mind, making her uncomfortable.

"Hi," Zion says, straightening up.

"And who sent you?" She asks.

"Michael." Zion answers.

She shakes her head.

Do they not know him?

"Well, we— Michael and I— were together, and there was shooting... he took the *vistigeum*— I'm not sure if he's made it out. He might be coming... I don't know." Zions rambles, thinking that her only witness is probably dead.

"Michael is fine." The woman clarifies. "But he did not send you." She holds up her hand to stop the questions from Zion. "You need rest. Everything else will come in time."

****

Zion wakes but doesn't open her eyes. *Maybe if I lay here, my dreams will become reality.* The lady in charge did say she needed to rest.

If only that incessant ticking would stop!

Zion snaps her eyes open and "Ah!" She crawls back into her bed to get some space from a pair of owl-shaped eyes.

"Twenty-six seconds." From this distance, Zion can see the person attached to the eyes. She is a small, Hershey-skinned girl, maybe in her late teens, with brown hair, which may have hints of red in the sunlight. She is beautiful, and her eyeglasses magnify her brown eyes, making her look cartoonish. "It took twenty-six seconds for you to open your eyes after waking." She continues.

"What?" Zion has so many questions but cannot form anything in her sleep haze.

"Your sleep pressure indicated that you had progressed from the sleep cycle to awake, but you did not seem to accept the change until right before you opened your eyes, which was 26 seconds." She informs as if she was asked.

It would have been longer if I had left in peace.

"I'm Khamira. Some people want to call me Kami, but only my friends can call me that. So don't."

Zion blinks, "Well then, Kami." At the younger girl's glare, she adds, "—rah. What are you doing here?"

She shrugs. "I was sent here because my mom knew a person who knew Kateri, and she sent me here." Zion learned that Kateri was the woman she met when she arrived yesterday. She's the one who organized this operation.

Khamira pulls out a small item that looks like a compact mirror and a little tool. She starts fixing it. Or maybe she is disassembling it? It doesn't matter.

"What I meant was, what are you doing in *here*? This room." Zion clarifies.

"Hmm, so many ways to answer. What makes us do anything?"

"Why—"

"The important people got some information, from me, I should add, and they want to figure out what to do with it. I was asked to leave. I've been told that I'm not good with sensitive information. But I know everything there is to know about everyone here, except you. Even though now I know it takes 26 seconds for you to accept awareness. That could be the difference between life and death. You should work on it."

Zion gapes at the little nymph (because she looks like a mythical creature with her big eyes and golden Afro).

"Wait, what are they discussing? What did you find out?" Zion gets out of bed and catches the towel that Khamira throws from somewhere.

"There's water next to your bed. We only have hot water for emergencies."

"Okay."

"I accessed footage from a FEMA camp. They're hoping that we can use it and communicate with someone there."

"Who is 'they'?" Zion asks.

"The important people." Khamira rolls her eyes. "Keep up."

The device in her hands clicks, and she smirks. After rolling something on the bottom of the small circle-shaped device, she hears sounds... no, voices.

"Welcome to the conversation," she tells Zion.

Zion changes her mind. *She's no nymph, and she's a mastermind.*

She starts to distinguish voices that she recognizes.

"How do we know who to contact? We reach out to the wrong person, and everything we have worked for goes kaboom." That sounds like the cowgirl.

There is a deep sigh and response, "We're going to follow Kateri's plan and listen. We can gather Intel and then decide who to contact." That sounds like Ravi: "We can get more information by keeping our heads down."

"We've kept our heads down!" Zion smiles to herself at Michael's passionate response. He really is okay. "Keeping our heads down has been causing us to be picked off individually. We've already lost Ayden and Dai last week. We need to do more!"

There is silence, and Zion looks at Khamira, who is staring into space, moving her lips like she is reading something. Zion looks over her shoulder but sees nothing. Still, before she can ask, Khamira twists something on the side of the Compact device, causing the silver screen to turn from black to an unclear image. After a couple more adjustments, it's visible.

"This is what they're seeing," Khamira explains.

Zion sees a group of men and women in what looks like a prison, covered in lime green jumpsuits. The wind is blowing strongly, and many of them have huddled together. A man stands before them, speaking with his face uncovered, while the other three people wear masks as they walk through the camp, keeping the people in line.

"What is this?" She asks.

"It's a FEMA camp. The leaders put the people who are a threat to their agenda here. These people are charged with disturbing the peace, acts of terror, and other things like that. We've heard of it, but this is the first time I could bypass their security and get footage."

The camera is viewing from what looks like the north side of the camp. She can see a food dispensing system and a building to the right, which may be a bathroom or shower area. There looks to be rooms in a large fortress which runs along the edge of the compound. There are young, old, and even some that look like older children.

One of the women she sees is helping another, handing her a jacket. She looks young and healthier than most. It's like she might have just got there. Zion smiles as she is reminded of her sister.

Wait.

That's Adria!

Zipporah Anderson

Chapter 13

$\mathcal{Z}$ion bursts into the hall just outside of her room. This one is covered in a different type of vine than the main chamber and has much more sunlight from various skylights. She turns her head back and forth, not knowing which way to go. The compact spy device — *dubbed by yours truly* — made it seem as if the group was right outside the door. This compound looks exactly the same in every direction.

"You should go left." She hears Khamira walk behind her. "The room is in the next hall, third door to the right." Zion had forgotten about her in her haste to get to the other room.

"Thanks," Zion says and rushes to follow the directions she was given. But, "it's a dead end." When she gets to the opening, it's a high ceiling with no plants or life, just cement... She looks all around, but it appears to be just a wall. She knows that she followed the directions, but maybe Khamira was mistaken. She never did look up from that compact spy device.

Zion turns around, looking for the fairy-like girl, and walks to the hallway to see her casually looking at her device and walking forward like a teen looking at their cell phone.

"You waited for me." She says when she sees Zion at the corner. "Is that because you think we are friends?"

"Well..." *I wasn't actually* waiting *for you.*

"They know we are here. Let's go in," Khamira says, finally looking up directly at the wall.

As if by her command, the door opens, reminiscent of the one she and Michael encountered on their first meeting.

They are now face-to-face with the frowning Ravi. "Now is not a good time." He says everything slowly as if he has to process it before anything is said.

"We're already aware of all that is transpiring inside the meeting. Our input would be valuable and should be considered." Khamira quickly responds, gesturing to her device and back to him.

"Khamira—" not *a friend,* Zion notes, "you're too young."

"If I'm too young, then I won't help you. At all." She shrugs.

Ravi squints his whiskey-colored eyes and opens his mouth to respond but is interrupted.

"Let them in." They hear Kateri call from within the room.

Khamira smiles brightly and clearly conveys, 'I told you so' without words as she enters the room.

"And you?" Ravi looks at Zion.

She steals herself for a fight. "I know you guys are looking into the camps. I don't know a lot, but my best friend is there. And you're not leaving me out of this conversation."

Ravi's expression changes to surprise.

"You know someone there? You saw them?" Ravi leads her into the room.

"Yes." She looks confused at his reaction, "Adria, She's like a sister. We were supposed to come here together, but... she sacrificed herself so I could escape. Is she OK? Can you see if anything happened to her?"

"First, look at the screen. Do you see her?"

Zion desperately hopes that looking at the larger image with more clarity does not disappoint her. It appears that that will be the case until,

"There! With the braid." While all of the people appear to be looking in the same direction as a maskless guard, Adria is scanning the peripheral area, and for just a moment, she faces the camera. Zion's eyes begin to fill. She is thankful that she is OK, but this camp reminds her of historical camps where survivors were hurt more than just physically.

"I didn't see it before, but that's definitely the woman who was with you." Zion turns to see Michael, and she gasps. He has a bandage on the right side of his neck and forehead, and his left arm is in a sling wrapped around his wrist. "Good to see you made it and are already a part of decision-making." He winks, and she smiles at him before turning to the screen again.

"So, what are we going to do?" she asks.

"We were discussing, trying to make contact or get a man on the inside so that we can infiltrate the camp to determine the enemies' next move and free these people," Chaz responds. "But now, with your friend inside, we can use her." She looks at Kateri for approval. "Right?"

"It would be ideal and has fewer lives at risk," Kateri says.

"Wait. Whose life is at risk?" Zion asks, feeling as if she is still not getting the whole picture.

Everyone except Khamira looks to Kateri, who is deep in thought. Finally, she breaks the silence.

"You cannot repeat what you are about to hear, even to others in The Hill." Zion is intrigued and nods along with everyone else. "I have received word that the *Portentum Change* has been implanted in 60% of the world's population. People have been herded toward the agenda and swallowed the propaganda. Once the acceptance rate is at least 75%, the leaders will activate it. Chemicals will be released into the bloodstream and nervous system, poisoning them from the inside.

"We have to put a stop to it. To warn people and help them. Abigor has enticed them with promises of freedom, identity, and scientific breakthroughs. But the people must not be fooled. The answer to your question is everyone. All of our lives are at risk."

Kateri stares into Zion's eyes as if reading her reaction to what she has heard. However, Zion hopes she is unaware of her thoughts because she doesn't understand them herself.

"I can create a communication device and drop it into the camp since we now have a contact there. We can then gather intel on the leaders' future plans and disrupt them." Khamira inserts herself into the conversation while sitting in a chair with the prisoners in front of the screen. She starts typing quickly, losing herself in her task. "Since I have limited equipment, I'll need a connector on the ground. Then we make nice with your friend and save the world."

That sounds great, but "she won't trust any of you." Zion voices.

"She may recognize me from the meeting with Johnathan," Michael says as he steps from his spot in the back corner of the room.

"You're injured." Zion points out. "It makes no sense to send you into what could be a death trap!"

"Well, you're not trained, and I'm the only other person she knows." He refutes, "In a situation like this, you could die."

"Like *you* nearly did." Zion hears Chaz snicker at her remark.

"If God says it's my time, then it will be."

"That doesn't mean you help Him!"

"As entertaining as this is, we need a decision," Chaz interjects, and even Khamira stops her typing to look at Kateri, waiting for her verdict.

Kateri closes her eyes in deep thought and lets out a long exhale. She opens them and appears to embody leadership as she speaks. "Michael, you will go to a mutual place and meet Jonathan. We'll get his take on the situation." Zion frowns. She doesn't like the vibe she gets from him. "As always, do not disclose sensitive information to him and tread carefully."

"What should I tell him? You know that he will require a trade if he helps us." Michael asks.

Kateri furrows her dark brows in thought.

"You can tell him about my mother. She knows a lot and is on the main team of people who created *The Change*. Her being in custody could be bad." Khamira volunteers. This is the second time she has brought up her mother, and Zion can't help but be curious. When she assesses everyone else, it appears that Ravi and Chaz are also clueless. Who is her mother?

Michael answers as if he could hear her thoughts. "LaQuinn Noble." He nods, "She has been integral to our success and safety. There's no way we could have gotten this far if she hadn't helped any of us. Including Johnathan. He'll definitely be interested, but I'm not sure that it's going to be good enough or if we should even volunteer that."

"Maybe you can tell him that Adria is in the camp. They have some— they were, uh, well... They know each other." Zion finishes awkwardly.

"Do you think that will convince him to accept a dangerous mission?" Ravi adds. "Is that enough?"

"I hope so," she responds.

"Very well, Ravi says, "let's plan."

****

"So, you will speak with Jonathan and his people. Prepare for anything. The last few meetings have not gone well. Ravi will watch you all from this location across the street." Khamira points to a spot on another digital map.

Zion, Chaz, and Mike are geared up in dark clothes with gloves and black shoe covers. Zion was called into the meeting because it was sensitive, and Kateri did not want too many people made aware of the information to avoid taking any chances for leaks.

"Are you wondering how I know all of this?" Khamira asks out of the blue.

"No."

"Umm…"

"Yeah, sure."

All three respond at once, and Khamira looks at Michael (the only positive answer) with a bright smile.

"You can tell me all about it later, Kami."

Is he *a friend?*

"Let's go, ladies. Kateri will be in touch."

Chaz and Michael have told Zion multiple times to follow and not say anything. They travel through the tunnels in silence. It doesn't seem like they're going very far before Michael reminds them to keep their eyes open and not worry about waiting around if anything happens…

"If no one trusts him, then why do we do business with him?" Zion asks after 10 minutes of silence.

Michael Hmms. "It is very difficult staying out of sight. We have around 15 people who need food and shelter at least. They are counting on us to make the right decisions for them. To protect them. Jonathan has more ability to move in inner circles, which is why we won't cut contact. We get a lot of information from him and vice versa. If it wasn't for the grace of God — "

"— or our usefulness." Chaz cuts in

"They would have eliminated us long ago. His group is double our size and more likely to take justice into their own hands."

"But that leads to people getting hurt, which is why I don't know why you're here," Chaz adds.

"How does me being here change anything?" Zion asks.

"Let's get one thing straight." Chaz stands all 5'1" of her height and looks the darker woman in the eye. "If you're caught up in a 'sticky situation,' I'm not going out of my way to save you. Got it?"

"I wouldn't put it past you to create a sticky situation for me in the first place."

"All the more reason." She smirks.

"Enough." Michael rolls his eyes. "We're *all* getting out of here." He takes a deep breath. "Let's go."

Chaz slams her hand into the wall, and the space in front of them lifts to reveal a small studio-sized, brightly lit room. There is no furniture or appliances except for a singular painting of a regal ship without a sail surrounded by People swimming in the ocean all around it crying out.

"Friends!" They hear as they step into the room. The three of them face a dozen armed men and women with Jonathan in the center. "Welcome." Despite his kind words and open arms, he looks very unhappy.

* * * * * * * * *

Zion never paid much attention to the changes in weapons until she found herself at the wrong end of a barrel for the nth time in so many days. She struggles to focus.

"Why the warm welcome?" Michael asks, pausing just inside the room.

Some time back, some important person started using air in those weapons. Something about pressure and water. It's supposed to have the same force as traditional gunpowder weapons. Zion hears them speaking, but her mind takes her elsewhere.

"Even you have to admit that it's suspicious that we've been located three times since our last meeting. I've lost good men!"

With the right amount of spin and power, these weapons can do so much damage that a single shot can make a person unrecognizable. They are even variable so that you can shoot a direct or wide shot with the same weapon.

"Sounds like you have a problem," Chaz says.

They promoted the weapons as cleaner because we want to save the environment with less mess.

"Well, I think it's time to get rid of the problem," Johnathan concludes.

Unless you count the blood and guts.

Zion feels Michael grab her arm and force her behind him, bringing her into awareness. Chaz is yelling and has pulled her own weapon out of... Somewhere.

Is there ever a time when you look death in the eye and are not afraid...

Chapter 14

"We're Going!" She hears Michael yelling toward the other side of the room, pushing her to the exit and making Zion push back.

"No! We can't leave! What about Adria!"

"Hold."

It's as if someone has pressed the pause button, and everyone is frozen. She feels herself breathing heavily, and she looks to see a dozen weapons aimed toward them. Michael has a grimace on his face, making himself appear much older as if a weight is settled on his shoulders. A peek at Chaz shows her with her weapon pointed at the opposition. At least it isn't pointed toward her. This time.

Zion is startled to see Jonathan coming through his soldiers as if parting a sea. He has a peeved look on his face, but it quickly turns into a charming smile.

He raises his hands to show that he is not armed, but Michael doesn't budge from his position between them.

"Call off your men," Michael demands.

"Technically, most of them are women." Johnathan jokes. He is not met with amusement, so he shrugs, "Stand down." Everyone lowers their weapons, and Chaz follows, though Zion doesn't think for a moment that she is unprepared to hit a target.

Michael steps aside, and Zion finds herself face-to-face once again with Jonathan. He really does have a charismatic way about him. He even smiles reassuringly as if the trio almost dying was only a dream. She has never trusted him, but Adria always has. And regardless of their past, her sister always returns to the scoundrel.

"You're her friend." Jonathan pauses in thought before finally continuing, "Zion." She fights the urge to roll her eyes at the dramatic man. He definitely knows who she is. They have known— and disliked— each other for years. "I see you're with the Holy Crew now and all alone."

She nods in response.

"What about Adria?" he repeats her earlier question, stepping closer, "Where *is* your other half?"

Zion feels Michael and Chaz have also stepped closer to her, but Johnathan's presence overwhelms her senses.

"A-Adria and I got separated. She was taken to a camp—" Her eyes cut to Michael, unsure how much they want to be shared "—when we met your guys, it was a trap, and she was taken. She trusted you!" She feels her anger begin to overtake her fear.

"I set no trap!" he roars back before containing himself. "It's funny that *you're* here with them, and she isn't. You seem to make friends fast, seeing as yesterday you didn't know anything, and now we've been hit twice, and your *friend* is gone."

"You think I have something to do with this?" Zion exclaims and prepares to defend herself.

"Our esteemed leader seems to think so." he interrupts firmly.

"What does that mean?" Chaz visibly loses patience in the conversation.

Jonathan pretends to think before deciding to share. He reaches into his pocket, and everyone tenses until he pulls out a flat, palm-sized disc that reminds Zion of Khamira's compact spy device. After a few touches, he finds what he is looking for.

Zion gasps when he turns the screen towards them.

"Is that— why is there a picture of me?" She asks the room but receives no response except for her own buttered chocolate eyes on an image looking over her shoulder. There is no mistaking that it's her.

"Congratulations, princess. You've graduated from being a fugitive to a wanted criminal. The only question left is, who'd you screw over to get there?" The question is loaded with accusations.

"I would never have given her over! You should know that!"

"I know you've gotten your hands on something the government doesn't want you to have! Now you can give it to me or..." he leaves it unsaid, but the weapon he pulls from his back, *I knew he was armed,* says it all. He doesn't even flinch at Chaz's gun, which, after a second, points to him.

There is a stalemate.

No one moves. Zion knows that she has nothing but is unsure if saying something will give away any advantage.

"Why don't we make an exchange?" Michael says, bringing the attention back to him as he walks to the middle of the room, drawing all the weapons in the room minus Chaz'. "We have something that you want."

"It may be easier just to kill all of you," Johnathan responds.

"If you really wanted to kill us, you would have." Michael challenges to Zion's displeasure. "You are here because you want information."

Zion's eyes flash as she recognizes him introducing the proposition that they previously discussed.

* * * * * * * * *

"He's going to want information. What can we tell him?" asks Ravi.

"We cannot disclose that we have video of the camp or where to find this Hill," Kateri says.

"He wants an inventor to create tools for him and his team," Michael suggests.

"You mean weapons for him and his team." Khamira clarifies.

"We can't allow that destruction." Kateri turns the idea down.

"So, what do we tell him?" Zion asks.

* * * * * * * * *

"We have access to data that you may find useful," Michael speaks quickly to deter yet another interruption. *Hook.* "We would need you to deliver something in the camp to disturb the communication signal. Anything that we even attempt before then would be detected and could end in catastrophe. For both of us." *Line.*

Jonathan nods and turns his back to them. "And what do I get for putting myself and my Allies at risk?"

"Ever heard of LaQuinn Noble?" *And sinker.* Johnathan abruptly turns around at the name with a gleam in his eye.

"Of course. She is one of the head scientists in the *Vistigeum* team and has been a leader in advancements of the *Portentum Change.*"

"Well, she got into some things that her colleagues disapproved of. She defected."

The smile that breaks out over his face gives him a youthful charm, and Zion almost expects him to start singing Christmas carols. Kateri was right; she knew he would be very interested in acquiring the scientist.

"We know her location and would be willing to share *if* you help us with our objective." Michael offers. There is a lapse of silence, which seems to be too much for Chaz.

"So, what will it be?" She asks.

"What are friends for? Looks like we'll be partners once again." he claps his hands together. "What's the mission?"

Theoretically, the plan is very simple.

Step one: Jonathan infiltrates the camp.

Step two: he plants the three circuit interrupters around the camp, allowing Step three.

Step three is for Khamira to drop a drone device to Adri.

Step four: Zion gets information from Adria about the people in the camp while Jonathan gets Noble out. (Before getting Adri out, there need to be more eyes on the inside so that they can plan a mass breakout).

Step five: Show the masses what's going on so that people can stop being brainwashed.

And finally, step six: get all those people out of there, and everyone can come together and sing Kumbaya until the end of the world.

All while not getting anyone killed. Simple, right?

Wrong. Zion tries not to panic at the thought of it all. There are so many ways that something can go wrong. *I should have taken notes. I always tell my students, when in doubt, to take notes.*

At the moment, they are all waiting. Only the people who know of the plan are in the room. (Besides Chaz and Ravi, who left after waiting two hours.) Zion considers going too to get away from the stress. Michael is pacing the floors, and Kateri sits with her eyes closed, occasionally checking Khamira's progress.

Minutes extend into hours. What if Jonathan and his goons don't follow through? They seem like the type to make their own rules.

"And the party has started." Khamira's mumbled words snap everyone to attention.

"Father." She looks more animated, whereas before, she moved leisurely. Now, there is purpose with each press of a button. "Spirit."

"Khamira, would you care to explain?" Kateri calmly asks. Saints would be jealous of this woman's patience.

"I guess." She shrugs as if everyone should know what she is thinking, "I named my bond jammers Father, Spirit and...." She waits for the third light on her screen to flash, "Son! Great. With these activated, the bonds in the facility's defense system can't communicate, which means that no one will notice my ETD— which, before you ask, is an encrypted transmission device— even if they fixed the bonds. The ETD is now a part of the grid, see?"

Definitely, do not see, Zion thinks while nodding in agreement.

"Now I can drop the communicator to your friend, and all *you* have to do," she looks at Zion, "is make sure she doesn't raise any alarms and give everything I worked for away."

"Where's Jonathan and his people?" Michael saves her from responding.

"The last ETD was placed on the far South side of the camp, which theoretically has the weakest defenses. He should let us know, if he follows the plan, when he gets to the internal layout." Michael scoffs, doubting that communication. "It's no biggie if he doesn't. My drone can see up to 50 miles away and has reflectors. I can map out their entire camp and find out where most people are within a couple of hours, depending on the size."

"Create the map. And we should make contact tomorrow," Kateri suggests. "Let's all rest before then, and I feel we will need it."

Zion holds her protest and is just grateful that the little genius is on their side.

* * * * * * * * *

Zion realizes as she walks the halls that evening that she has never had time to explore The Hill. Doing so now, she can see why it has earned its name. Each of the walkways are angled down at a slope. Try eventually converge together in a valley. At the center is a subterranean lake, which looks like a natural cavern with Hard Rock and algae around the perimeter. There are lit lanterns on hangings, giving it an ethereal feel.

This place is what peace. No human could have created it.

There is a gentle sound of falling water, which she identifies as a slow falling waterfall, which gently disturbs the silence. But she doesn't mind. She sits and feels as if the falling water teases her tear ducts, and they begin to overflow in jealousy. This is the first time she has been still and quiet enough to feel. So, she releases the torrent of emotions held back by unsettled dams.

Before she knows it, she is sobbing in mourning as if from grief. She misses her grandmother, who passed away only five years prior, directly before the creation of The World Alliance. She raised her like a mother when her own passed away from cancer.

Her father was an immigrant from Jamaica and was deported when she was eight years old.

She felt that her granny was too restrictive and left home for college only to never see her again.

She misses teaching when kids were carefree and didn't have to worry about whether they would live another day. She misses Adria, who is her sister in every way that matters.

Why couldn't they both be here? Why did she have to go to that terrible camp? Why is the law searching for *her*? There must be hundreds of people who've run away before. Why don't her choices matter?

The tears and sobbing don't seem to have an ending, and Zion doesn't even know who she's frustrated with anymore! So many questions were never answered. Why? Why? Why!

"I have asked that question many times myself." Zion turns quickly to find that she is not alone. "Sometimes, I get an answer, and others not."

"Let me guess, God answers you."

"Yes and no. We have a long-standing relationship and understanding, God and me. I don't always need an answer." Kateri takes a seat next to Zion on her rock. She reminds Zion of

Grandmother Willow from the traditional children's movie Pocahontas.

"Have you looked around?" Zion yells. If she wants to invade her anger, then she can deal with it. "Why are so many bad things happening? You all seem so sure you'll win, but your people are dying daily! I don't feel what you're feeling. That security. In what? It doesn't make sense from what I see. It feels like you use the Bible and God as a crutch for anything you can't explain. Or to justify what you *want* to be true. You don't believe in the Alliance, so you start a rebellion, and now here I am on a wanted list like a criminal. How do you justify that? I'm listening. Make me understand how any of this is worth it!"

Zion breathes heavily, realizing she is standing, and her voice has risen. "I'm sorry. That wasn't...You've all been very kind to me. I shouldn't have—I didn't mean to offend."

"It is not offensive to have questions, child." Kateri stands and looks into Zion's eyes and she drops them in shame. Kateri places a hand gently on each side of the younger woman's face. "I see your struggles and your pain, and as much as I wish it to be so, I cannot take it away. But I know who can."

Zion shakes her hands off and steps back. "I can't be this perfect person like you. Turning my back on all of my mistakes and judging others for theirs. Waiting for a Savior and sacrificing my body in the hope that my soul *might* make it to a fanciful place where I don't have any control over myself. Where I turn my back on my family and friends if they disagree with me. I just can't."

Kateri nods and closes her eyes, breathing calmly as if meditating. She begins to walk away, and Zion doesn't call her back but finds she doesn't want to be alone. "Would you come with me? I'd like you to see something."

"Okay." Zion hesitates but follows her when she walks away from the cavern. Kateri has mastered the look of one who is firm but kind. She is very nurturing, the type of mother that Zion imagines in fairytales. One that you do not want to anger and hang on every word spoken.

When they slow, they turn into a moonlit escape. The large room has plants and flowerbeds with fruit trees and vegetables, *which explains the stew for dinner twice.* The entire area is covered with some sort of greenery. It is like a natural greenhouse. Looking up, Zion can see small birds snoozing on high branches.

"It is beautiful," she whispers as if her very voice will disturb the atmosphere.

"Yes. My son and I began cultivating this place three years ago, and it has thrived."

She continues before Zion can ask more about her son, "Look at the plants. At the trees. Do you see how they bloom even in this place where they were never meant to be? Look how strong they are, with deep roots strengthening them. They are all so unique and have much purpose." She looks at Zion meaningfully as if trying to impart something into her mind.

"I'm sure they do," Zion responds to fill the silence.

"They are beautiful, but there is much to learn from them. And they make great listeners." She smiles, "but not as good as people it would seem."

"Huh?"

Kateri looks over her shoulder, and after a second, Chaz, Ravi, and another little boy, no older than twelve who introduces himself as David (Ravi's younger brother) step from the wall, which hid them from sight.

"Sorry," Chaz says, not sounding apologetic at all. "Was just curious."

"I am not angry." Kateri responds, "Join us."

They all sit beneath the shade of the tallest tree, and Kateri starts again. "Zion, I brought you here because your emotional words shamed me and exposed me. Not because I feel that they pertain to me or anyone else here but because I know more than most about those who stay in the Hill and their challenges and beliefs. However, I have not been open about my life and what convicts me to Christ and the Adherens. I want all of you to know that I am not perfect."

It is remarkable to believe in something so much that you would die for it.

"I know that you have not been here long, but eight others stay in the Hill." Kateri addresses Zion more than the others since they know the people here in the Haven. "Two are children, 15 and 12, and the others are very young as well. Some I even raised in adoption or foster care. They are all my children."

"But your son? Did you not birth any children?" Zion interrupts and then blushes at her forwardness.

"No. But I never wanted any. I wanted to live my life traveling and enjoying the finer things I could access." She chuckles, "I felt like I couldn't have a relationship with God because of my other relationship preferences. I couldn't understand a God who would send someone to hell for disagreeing with Him, especially when no one was hurt. But many areas in my life didn't align with the Bible's teachings."

"Like what?" David asks.

"For one, I was proud and didn't believe that there needed to be restrictions on your money, who I chose to have relations with, what you eat and drink, and things like that. And I knew that my choices and my sexual preferences specifically, were said to be an abomination to God. Why would I want to follow Him? There was no reason for me to compromise my lifestyle when it wouldn't matter anyway."

"So, how do you end up here? With the children and being a... follower? I'm not sure what to call you," Zion says bashfully, and Kateri laughs a beautiful sound.

"That's not entirely your fault," Ravi explains, "Christians became too religious a name, and Believer was vague; terrorist and radical are untrue. The term Adherens is adequate, but it is a term often associated with a fanatical religious person. I think "follower" is good." *Wow, that was a lot of words to agree.* Zion thinks she will hold all questions from here on out, though no promises.

"Thank you, Ravi." Kateri continues, "We are followers of The Way. There is only one truth." Kateri inhales deeply and warms her hands in front of her. She looks excited, like someone with a secret they can't wait to tell. Zion leans forward in anticipation.

One of the promises that The World Alliance promoted was that all truths would be accepted. No one could tell you that you are wrong except for the absolutes. Kateri believes the exact opposite.

"I had everything that I thought I needed. Family, finances, success, and love. The American dream. One day, I came across a young man, who I later found out was a large 14-year-old, who looked at me in a sparsely populated park, smiling from his position on a park bench. I smiled back but walked into another man who asked me for money. He was dirty and aggressive, so I looked at him in judgment and turned him away. But then, I see this kid reach into his pocket, give the man dollar bills, and *then* give him his jacket! In January in DC!

"So, I approached the kid afterward, wondering where his parents were because he must have someone to buy him another one. I found out that he had lost his entire family in a car crash a month prior and was in the foster care system. I felt ashamed and convicted. That was the start. I know you are waiting for the story of an angel who spoke from heaven to tell me what the truth was, but I researched for myself. I read the Bible when it was still legal, of course. I wanted to hate it and say it was untrue because it didn't fit into my life, which was perfect in my mind. Still, I fostered and later adopted that boy, followed by many others.

"The life I live now offered me something that I never could have gotten. Freedom, peace, happiness, love. I did have to say goodbye to some things and give up some others. But I could never use the Bible to justify my wants. I am in a relationship with Jesus Christ and truly want to live with him. I've probably overshared, but I stopped looking at my position as a mother and leader to mean that I had to be perfect because I am not. So do not feel as if you must look down on others to know God. He is strong in our weakness. Our imperfections make us who we are, but He loves us anyway."

"Ravi went to jail for two years because he made fake money and stole a lot of stuff. And he talks about Jesus stuff all the time." David pipes in, and Ravi blushes before fondly cuffing the kid.

"Don't mind him," he says, ignoring the shout of protest for his brother. "He can be very disobedient at times."

"I am not!"

"Well, I like liquor and men," Chaz adds her two cents. "And I am prone to violence. I am quick to lie, especially when in a stupid situation. I also lash out when I'm nervous. Sorry about before, by the way." Zion smiles at her, and she continues. "I may or may not have sticky fingers, and..." Her tone changes to one of regret, "I hurt someone very close to me and then met someone who balanced me out. I held onto it for so long and didn't even realize the trauma I took into every area of my life. I can't say that I've let it go but I'm tame now." *This is her tame?* "I'm glad you opened up Kateri."

Zion smiles at their stories. She has so many more questions, and Kateri smiles back at her as if reading her mind.

"It is okay to have questions, Zion, and those questions, being angry; it is normal. But if you truly have an open mind and an open heart, you will know the truth. For just like there is one way, there is only one truth. If you seek, you will find."

Zion nods her head and really thinks. Kateri didn't really give her any answers. It reminded her of her grandmother's response to what *insert word here* means.

"Look it up." But maybe the answer is closer than she thinks.

Chapter 17

"Let's go over it again." Zion ignores the unsubtle groans of Khamira, Chaz, and Michael and focuses on Ravi, who simply nods and begins again.

"We need you to make contact and ensure your friend does not sound the alarm. She already knows and trusts you, so you will do most of the talking unless something arises. There's an area on the far southeast side of the camp opposite what may be their sleeping quarters. We need her to check for a possible entry point. From our calculations, Jonathan and his people are still in the area. If any contact with him is noticed, we need to know his intention but proceed with caution. The objective is to determine if there is a way in and out. And where the missing people are being kept."

"Okay, and she is listening for names: Noble, Khamira, Adherens, Jonathan, and... mine," Zion adds to which Ravi nods.

They need as much information as they can get from this because they need to get everyone out as soon as possible to save the most lives.

"Now, before we have to go over everything for a *fourth* time," Khamira rolls her eyes, "let's do this."

Zion can't understand her enthusiasm; Ravi and Kateri explained this mission's risk, and they will all be caught if anyone finds the comm device (Khamira says it's her version of a HEDY, whatever that is). Her sister could be killed or tortured for information she doesn't even have!

Deep breaths, no need to freak out. Zion tells herself.

"The drone is in place. It's still dark, so I should be able to drop the device as soon as we see Adria."

Kateri predicted that they would expel the prisoners early in the morning because having them in the open is easiest for the 11 guards monitoring the area. That reminds Zion of the slight possibility that one of them will notice the insect-sized communicator headed to her friend.

As predicted, men and women emerge from two doors on the north side of the camp. Everyone lets out a breath of relief when their target is spotted halfway through the crowd. She looks at the man in the line beside her out of the corner of her eye like he is a strange sight despite everyone wearing the same forest green jumpsuit.

Khamira has a small remote and guides what looks like a flying spider from the spot directly across from the rooms. There is a small dot with a blinking light on a map that Khamira created of the camp overnight.

"10 feet away," she says casually, not taking her hands or her eyes from the task. "When the device is planted within her hair, it'll crawl towards her nape. The volume is loud enough, but only for 25 seconds. I have to keep the frequency low so that nothing unusual is noticed. She has to plant it herself. If she can follow directions, then this won't all have been a waste."

Zion has practiced the conversation a hundred times, but things rarely happen the way you practice. Still, she centers herself and gets ready for her task. *Please, please, please let this work.*

"I'm in position and... coming around."

"Wait! What if she swats it?"

"Ready."

Zion exhales forcefully and presses the button. It feels like the ones in movies that make things blow up.

"Adri is me. Act normal, and don't panic."

Khamira really is a genius. She even thought of making contact when Adria had turned to walk alone so no one would see her jump in fright and put her hand to her ear, quickly covering the movement by tucking her hair behind her ear.

"Zy?"

"Yeah. Who were you expecting?" Zion gives a watery chuckle.

"I don't understand...how—"

"Before I say anymore, I need you to take the little bug from your nape. You should feel "skin" on your fingers. Run it along the bridge of your ear."

Adria scratches her hair to find the bug. The time has passed, so she won't be able to hear her again until she plants the internal nano bug. However, the mic still works, so they hear her grumbles of "Where is it?" and "It's not a *bug* bug, is it?"

"I've got it!" Adria whispers just as Khamira nods, pulling the footage connected to the tiny cam

"Okay, can you hear me?" Zion checks.

"Yeah." Adria goes and sits along the far wall and covers her mouth as if she is cold. "I'm so glad you're okay. I didn't see you brought in, so I didn't know if I was more worried or relieved."

"I am okay. My muscles are sore, and my hair desperately needs TLC, but I found a group of good people. Have you heard anything about The Adherens?"

"Yeah. Since I've been here, they seem to be pretty popular. Two people were supposed to be associated with them. One lady would speak out all the time and sing spiritual songs. The men and women will gather around to hear her stories of hope. I don't know her name, though They took her away soon after I arrived. She hasn't come back."

Michael announces her name is Dai.

"I wish I had better news and time to catch up, but we need help. We want to get you all out of the enemy's hands and let people know there is way more than they understand going on, but that would bring us a lot of attention. Everyone would be in a lot of danger. Especially you." Zion informs her, saddened by the news of a woman she has never met.

"Well, I've got news too. One of Jonathan's friends is here. I think he goes by Wan. He recognized me and said there won't be a "here" much longer. So, whatever you're planning, I hope it'll happen fast. He's investigating something, sneaking around the camp. He's been here since last night." Adria sighs and smacks her head, "I think you were right. Johnny... his entire operation is a little backward. Wan wasn't *at all* surprised to see me and told me that my 'boyfriend' said hello."

Zion pauses before responding and looks at those in the room, raising her eyebrow in question. Kateri shakes her head in the negative. She frowns because she doesn't want Zion to share any information about their dealings with Jonathan. She doesn't like keeping secrets from her.

"I don't trust him, as you know." Zion honestly states. "Just keep your eyes open, okay?"

Adria nods her head. "So, what do you need me to do? You said you needed help, right? I'm ready. I feel like half of the people who rebel do it because of boredom. You're really saving my life here."

"This is going to be dangerous, Adri." Zion scolds, making her friend sigh.

"I know. Just lay it on me."

"We need... a lot." Zion frowns, not knowing where to start. "Okay, try to see if you can get information on where the people who disappear are taken. We also have to determine what general knowledge anyone has on some key things: Adherens, Khamira, Noble, Jonathan, and... me."

"Who would know you? Has something happened?"

"Uh—"

"Oh! I know one of those!" She interrupts herself before Zion can respond, which is good because, once again, Kateri is shaking her head in the negative. "A lady, Something Noble, was brought in, and there was a lot of fuss. Most of the people here were outraged that she created *The Change*, and others were glad to have her help. She was taken away very quickly, but everyone still talks about her." Michael asks Zion to relay a question about what people are saying, but Zion is frozen.

Someone is approaching her. A guard.

"Oh no." They are going to be caught. "Adri..."

"You there." He grunts, and Adria tilts her head in confusion. The camera lifts further to see more of the imposing figure in front of her. Her head moves right and left as she turns her head, looking for who they can mean. The guard is wearing the general face mask like one used for fencing: dark black and daunting. He doesn't repeat himself, only stares at Adria.

"Who?" His mask twitches and Zion can tell that he is not in a tolerating mood, even without seeing his face. Annoying people is like a not-so-hidden talent for that girl.

"Come with me."

"Just to be clear," Adria starts, still remaining in her spot seated in the corner. "'You there' referred to me here?" Zion is sure that if she were able to discern a facial expression, she is sure that she would see a very scornful man. "Why?"

"Come. With. Me."

"Don't push his buttons, Adria," Zion says quietly. Even though she knows he can't hear her, she turns around to downcast faces. That sounded like a last warning. He didn't even use his monotone voice that time. *I knew that they weren't robots.*

 "Is she going to be okay?

No response.

"Do they know about the HEDY?"

Nothing

"What are they going to do?"

They all look sympathetic as if they know what's coming but don't want to speak it.

"What are *we* going to do? What's plan B!" Zion sits roughly, dejected, as panic starts to set in.

"Well, this should be fun." she hears Adria say as she follows the guard, and Zion puts her head into her hands, muttering repeatedly.

"What did I do?"

Chapter 18

Heavy Gray eyelids investigate the room, waiting for his guest.

Paul frowns as he sees the shadow guard (cloned as the others in all black) roughly shove her down and push her into a chair. Her wrists are shackled, and she immediately starts to look around using her whole head and not simply her eyes. She looks at the "door" several times as it has now blended into the walls, making the room feel like an enclosed box. In the heat of the moment, when he saw her before, he didn't have time to observe her.

Now, looking at her, he is nixing his first thought that he had encountered a couple of girls in the wrong place at the wrong time. Looking at her in the present, she has a look of guilt. Like one who is determined not to change her mind or give in. When she allowed her friend to escape, Paul knew she was strong. But her face shows one who has faced many challenges. He knows because he shares the same look.

Paul decides that he has studied from a distance long enough and walks into the room.

The subject's eyes quickly flick toward him and read him from head to toe. A lesser man would blush, but he knows that she recognizes that he is the real threat in the room, even with the guard behind her. He waves the shadow guard away, and only the two are left in the room. They make eye contact.

"So…" she starts, "this is a bit excessive, isn't it?"

Paul feels his lips quirk upward, remembering their first interaction. He shrugs and reaches into his pocket for a stick of gum, offering it to her.

"It's protocol." She looks at him, the stick of gum, and back at him.

"Why would I take that?"

"The food here sucks," he deviates from the script, "thought you may enjoy some variety."

She pauses, thinking before shaking her head

Smart. She doesn't trust him. She'll proceed with caution.

"Adria Stone—"

"*Ah*-Dree-Uh," she corrects him, and he raises his eyebrow.

"Okay then, Miss Stone." He says, ignoring her frown at his lack of correction. "Your accomplice got away." *No surprise,* Paul notes, "and she joined with a group of terrorists who call themselves Adherens. Ever heard of them?"

She hums and leans back. "I'm afraid not. But since you mentioned her, what else do you know about my friend?" She questions.

"Friend?" He points out, thinking of how much he should share. "I don't remember saying you were friends."

Her brown eyes roll. "You know, small, dark-skinned, teary disposition. You spent hours chasing her a couple of days ago."

Paul's face remains unchanged, but his mind ignites. How would she know details about her friend's adventure and escape unless she was told? Has she made contact?

This one girl could be the missing link. This just became much more interesting.

"That does ring a bell." he responds, "Zion Freeman?"

"Yes. But you knew that. What do you *think* you know about her and that group?"

Paul puts away his good cop persona and firmly states, "I know that you know more than you should. What I want to know is how?"

"I don't—"

"Now. Is your only chance to comply." Paul has had many difficult interrogations but has never been more invested in an outcome. There is no time to coddle anyone. "You will not get another."

* * * * * * * * * *

Zion recognizes him from her chase and feels her chest tighten in anxiety. "This is bad guys. He—"

Beep! Beep! Beep!

"Yeah, No kidding!" Khamira rapidly starts to press the buttons on the pad in front of her and touch her screens, which are all flashing in warning with a red, hazy outline. Everyone is immediately alert.

Kateri adopts a commanding presence that Zion has yet to see from her. "Ravi, Chaz, quickly bring everyone to the evacuation quarters." They both run to do as ordered. "Khamira, go to the main room in case we need to exit quickly. Keep an eye on things and get the contingency in place. You know what to do. No evidence remains. Keep your eyes open. There is no room for mistakes." Khamira nods and pulls Zion into the chair she previously occupied.

"If you see a green X on the screen, you have 30 seconds until I disable, so follow Kat and get out of here." Without waiting for a response, she leaves the room.

"What is happening?" Zion can't hold her tongue anymore. Kateri glances at her but apparently decides to deal with her later because she walks over to Michael, who looks resigned.

"I hate to ask you to go. Again." Kateri places her hands on both of Michael's cheeks.

"I can handle it. And I always come back." He responds, gripping her hand in reassurance.

"That doesn't mean that you always will." She chastises.

"Then my time here will be done. You have taught me everything I need to know. I'll use it now."

"Go, my son." She takes her hands away and steps back with tears in her eyes.

"This is not goodbye, mom. I'll see you soon."

She nods. "No heroics. Get intel and return for evacuation."

He looks at the two of them, "There are two go-packs beneath the far bench. Make sure you get out of here."

And then it is just the two of them. Kateri finally begins explaining Zion as she walks over to get the packs.

"The Hill has been breached."

"What!" Zion stands.

"Sit down," Kateri commands in a voice that brokers no argument. "Don't run when you see a demon; it'll only chase you harder. We still have a job to do." Zion retakes her seat and waits for her next instruction. It is easier to stay centered on Kateri's strength. "They have only found the outer ring of the Hill, and we have precautions in place to protect us. We must get as much information as we can. Are you with me, Zion?" She can feel her eyes widen until they hurt, but she nods her head.

"I am. I'm with you."

"Good. Now listen." she points to the screen. "We need to know how we were found, and if anyone shared that information, everyone is still in danger."

Zion relays a question to Adria, who sits back. There seems to have been some back and forth between her and officer Paul that they missed, and Adri is no longer handcuffed.

I don't know how she managed that.

"—a violent branch of the Adherens." Paul is saying.

"I've already told you that Zion is not the type to hurt anyone."

He sighs and rubs his face. This is the most emotion Zion has seen with him. He seems confused and desperate before schooling his features. "My father always expected me to be in this occupation. It's what my family always did. But I wanted to help people. I still do." He sighs again, and Zion worries after his health. A little. "I can't do that if I have nothing to work with. Give me something." He begs.

"Okay." He sits up straighter at her answer. "But first, do you know where the Adherens are hiding? Are they in danger?"

The pause that overtakes the room is tense, and after almost a full minute, Paul finally says, "They are in danger. But not from me." Zion can see Adria's hands fist on the table, and she waits.

"What will you do now, Miss Stone? Will you let your friend die or help me?"

Zion frowns. *What does he know?*

Adria opens her mouth to respond, but it does not register in Zion's head because a large green X appears on the screen."

Kateri interrupts her shock.

"Time to go, dear."

* * * * * * * * *

Zion picks up the mic, "We've been breached." Adria jumps at the sudden sound in her ears. "I'll contact you if I can. Remember, even if you close your eyes, I'll still be here."

"Now, Zion," Kateri says before she receives a response. "We have to go."

She quickly gets up to follow and whispers a quiet "Be safe" just as the screen turns black.

The hall seems like a walk to the gallows. Well, more like a brisk Jog. As they go down the hallways, Kateri hits every other wall underneath heart-shaped vines. Zion can see a strong shot of electricity cover the entire wall before a small magnet falls off. As she goes by, she sees a symbol carved on it and the third time it happens, she picks the interest up and pockets it.

At the next intersection, Kateri stops and thinks. Before Zion can ask, '*Are you lost?*' Kateri shoves the two bags that she is carrying into Zion's arms. One is a small backpack similar to the first that Michael gave her, and the other looks like a small satchel with a disk that shines an ethereal blue. It has a similar symbol as the

197

one on her pendant. It's almost like three trumpets angling around each other. She thought it was an A but now she isn't so sure. She reaches her hand inside and—

"Ow! What is this?" She doesn't get any response because Kateri is on the move again. This time, the pace is much less frantic but still very fast. After a few feet, she sees why they have slowed. They return to the escape, which now has a podium in the center shaped like a half circle with Khamira in the center.

There are four screens spaced evenly apart and pads holding keys she is swiping and typing at. When they enter, the pair sees Khamira changing the image on one screen, and the others are all black. She moves things on the screen and then looks down at something. Zion walks up and sees that it is the size of a stress ball.

"They haven't found their way into the main compound, but they have surrounded the area. There are shadow guards everywhere. And I don't know where Michael is. Everyone else has evacuated through the pool." This is the first time that she has seemed unsure and young.

Kateri nods. "If you cannot make it work, then we will proceed without it."

"I just need more time." Khamira defends. "It works, but not from a distance. And the timer only lasts 5 seconds. It defeats the purpose."

"We need to leave immediately," Kateri says to her, though it looks like Khamira is in her own world.

"We don't have time to seal the passages. Khamira!" She finally gets the young girl's attention. "When everyone is out of the compound, we will head to the landing and then the bridge. We need to follow the others." They all jump at the sound of a thump behind them and turn around on high alert.

Michael is back and looks to have run around the entire Hill.

"Sound plan. We should move quickly though. I went to the outer ring and saw some demolition equipment. I don't think our guests are very friendly." He says, slightly out of breath.

"We've done all we can do," Kateri says to Khamira, taking the stress ball from her hands.

"Well, let's get out of here," Zion says.

Chapter 19

The quartet head down the long halls leading to the pool.

Boom!

Everybody drops, though that instinct will not protect them if the walls collapse. They look around, shaken by the loud noise. It is suddenly becoming very smoky, and instead it clearing over time, it becomes thicker, causing everyone to cough. Zion shakes her head because she can feel herself getting dizzy. She hears the others speaking but can't determine what they are saying. She drops to her knees and blinks rapidly.

"I...I can't..." Her tongue feels like lead, and she can't even panic as she feels something cover her mouth and nose.

They've caught us, Zion thinks. She tries to shake her head from side to side, fighting her assailant who is forcing something over her mouth and nose.

"Breathe, it's me." The words and voice don't register, and she keeps trying to push them away.

"Zion." She feels her chin held and turned to the right. "Look at me. Relax and breathe the oxygen." She sees Michael's hazel eyes level with her brown ones. He must notice the clarity return to her because he smiles. "Glad to see that you *can* follow directions, darling."

"Don't call me darling," Zion slurs, rolling her eyes over to the other pair to see Khamira wearing an oxygen mask and looking how Zion feels. Both Kateri and Michael have scarves, which may be made of a microfiber material covering their mouth and noses.

"Sounds like they took a shortcut," Michael says, and Kateri nods.

"We've got to get to the pool and block the passage."

"Split up." Khamira sputters out, looking nauseous, "If they are using infrared equipment, it's more difficult to utilize if we separate."

"Okay, little one, you're with me," Kateri says to her, taking half of her weight. Though the motion seems to make Khamira's dark skin paler, she does not protest.

"I don't like this," Michael says, helping Zion up. She is relieved that she does not feel as bad as Khamira looks.

"We must. Now go"

"Fine."

They are moving, but Zion looks back after them and feels very uneasy. *What if those two are caught? Or what if we are?*

She sighs in relief as the peaceful pool comes into view, an oxymoron to the tense environment. Michael approaches the weathered rock and presses his hand to it, making another platform appear. After pressing a combination of six, it declines back into a typical rock.

"See those boats?" Zion looks over her shoulder and sees three boats that are overturned and wet like they just surfaced. "We'll be ready to travel as soon as the—"

Boom!

The ground shakes even worse than before. And much closer.

"Look, darling." Zion jumps in fright, not realizing that he moved so close. "Two minutes and leave. Lower the latch once you're secured in the boat, and it will autopilot you out."

"Where are you going?"

"I have to go and help them."

Zion balks. "Help them how? You could get *yourself* killed, and that won't help anyone. You're not thinking."

"I don't have time to think!" he yells, revealing how worried he is, "Or explain." He faces her and looks her up and down, making her squirm. His calloused hands reach for her wrist and turn it upward. In her hand is the mask that he gave her only seconds earlier. *I don't remember taking it off.* "Keep this on. We don't know what gas is in the air, and I don't want you hurt. Or worse."

"I don't want *you* hurt." Zion whispers.

He pulls their hands to her face and places the mask there instead of answering. His hands hover over the edge of the mask, and she can feel the whisper of his heat. "Two minutes." He turns her by her shoulders toward the escape and firmly presses her forward.

"I—" Before Zion can continue to argue, he has already started back into the Hill. Since he gave her his oxygen mask, he only has his scarf.

Zion looks after him and then glances at the boats. And back and forth again.

What should she do?

Going back and getting killed won't help anyone! But leaving them behind would destroy her.

"This is not a good idea," Zion murmurs to herself, and she follows after Michael.

Unlike before, she can barely see anything past her outstretched hands. The skylights are all closed, and there is a gray haze in the air, which Zion assumes is the gas that made her dizzy earlier. Michael sprinted forward, but Zion continues at a snail's pace, and she feels like she will never catch up at this rate.

How far did he go? Where are the others?

She hears screaming and a yell, followed by the sound of thunder. She backs away from the sound, though it is overtaking her senses. Still, she moves much quicker than she advanced.

Coward, she thinks. She couldn't save Adria, and now these people will die. And she is doing nothing. No. Even worse, she does what she always does.

Run.

* * * * * * * * *

"Unh!" She finally turns the boat over and off the track that held it to the others. It looks as if it can fit about five men. There is a silver latch that disrupts the dark wood. But should she get rid of the other boats so she isn't followed? Not for the first time, she feels as if she is missing so much information.

A boom of thunder startles her so badly that she falls over.

She'll leave the boats. That way, Michael and the others can have an escape, too.

She really doesn't want to find out what's causing that noise. She starts pushing the boat out but pauses in relief.

"Come on!"

They're back!

Michael is dragging a distracted Khamira, who is fidgeting (again) but matching Michael's much longer stride. "We can make it!"

"Quickly!" Kateri comes into view not far behind them with the look of a fearless warrior. Zion makes a mental note to ask her more of her story. She is the personification of the strength that she wishes she had.

Zion spares a second to breathe but blanches when there is the marching sound of dozens of boots hitting the ground in one direction. This one.

"It's not enough, they're too many! We can't escape," Khamira shouts.

Another roll of thunder. No. It is the sound of the building screaming. They are destroying the Hill.

"We will!" Michael encourages between breaths.

Zion counts the seconds that it takes for them to reach her.

1

It feels as if they are moving in slow motion.

2

"We can do this!" Michael encourages.

3

The sound of gunfire and people yelling over one another is too close for comfort

4

Kateri looks over her shoulder as armed guards come into view just yards behind them.

5

Soldiers, both with and without masks, round the corners behind her friends. There are dozens of people marching, encouraging the building's terror.

6

Michael and Khamira come through the opening first, and he shoves her forward directly into Zion.

7

Zion starts to follow Khamira toward the boats, but she realizes that Kateri hasn't emerged.

8

She pauses Khamira and turns around to encourage Kateri, but...

9

The woman has stops moving and looks peaceful as if she is meditating.

She opens her eyes and looks at the trio with a knowing smile. She always smiles, as if she is on the right end of a secret.

"For every beginning, there must be an end." It's as if the soldiers have paused. Or time has. "My children. Always love and forgive." Her voice seems to echo and reverberate on the walls around her.

"No!"

Michael starts running back toward her, but she is several yards away from the opening where they stand.

"I love you. My son." She whispers, but it carries. Zion wonders if the wind will always hold her love.

Guards are steps away from overtaking her, and weapons are pointed toward the trio outside of the Hill.

Kateri holds her hand high and in it there is Khamira's stress ball.

Said girl makes an anguished sound and time speeds up. Zion realizes that she stopped counting.

Kateri squeezes the ball once and throws it to the ceiling. She smiles.

10

Zipporah Anderson

Chapter 20

Ringing. Or is it hissing?

Zion's eyes blur as she looks around to find the source of the sound. It's like a forgotten teapot.

"What—what happened?" She wants to speak more, but noise joins the initial ringing like another pitch attempting at harmony but off-key. Music? No.

Screams.

Zion shakes her head to clear it as she comes back into focus. Blinking furiously, she sees Khamira with her hands on a wall of fallen rocks and boulders. She is pushing and pulling desperately, but with every rock she repositions, another takes its place. Looking closer, Zion sees that it is debris from...

"Oh no." Zion breathes.

Kateri bombed the roof of the entrance to the cavern. The whole thing collapsed.

She's gone.

Zion feels tears gathering in her already burning eyes. It seems impossible for such a beautiful, strong soul to just be no more. Listening closer, she can hear occasional words through Khamira's screams.

"Kateri! Please don't— please!" Zion sees her banging on the newly made wall to move the barriers to her distress. Even from her distance, Zion can see blood falling down her arms from her hands.

She tries to get up and stumbles, losing the battle for balance, but seeing the young girl's anguish, she succeeds again. Barely.

As she moves over to Khamira, she is reminded that they were not alone.

"Wait." She pauses, "Where is Michael?" When she gets no response, she quickly approaches the hysterical teen and turns her so that their bodies face each other. Khamira immediately tries to turn back and assault the barrier again, but Zion holds firm.

"Khamira, listen to me." She shakes her shoulders, "Listen!" Zion's heart breaks at the pain in her eyes. No 15-year-old should have such eyes. "Where is Michael?"

Her question seems to make her crumble, and only her hands on her shoulders keep her upright.

"He was—he was right here. He was running and..."

"And what happened?" Zion fears for her answer.

"This is all my fault." she starts to tremble. Zion has no idea how much time has passed, but they must leave.

She refocuses her with another small shake, and as much as she doesn't want to, she asks, "Where is he, Khamira?"

She points a shaking finger perpendicular to the boats where a single figure lay.

"He's dead."

...

Zion doesn't immediately process what she just heard. *Dead?*

In her shock, she releases her charge and she sobs so hard that Zion fears for her ribs. She turns away in the direction of the crumbled body of Michael.

She fights not to get swallowed by grief.

He must have gotten hit by the blast when he went to try to save his mom. She heads over with anxiety. How can she look at him like this? First Kateri and now Michael.

She feels as if her heart is beating differently like it takes more effort for each muscle contraction.

Never being able to see his confidence or hear him defend people with passion. *Why would his God allow this to happen?*

Zion reaches him and touches his face, which still has heat, so it must not have been too long. Water is falling from somewhere onto his face, so she wipes it only to have more drops. She looks up but doesn't see anything.

Her eyes. They are overflowing. She doesn't feel her face falling or feel the urge to sob. She doesn't have the energy to do anything. But despite her telling herself that she cannot feel any more hurt, her emotions are rolling over in waves out of their hidden depths in her tear ducts.

She sinks her forehead into his bloodstained shirt. She wants to hide away.

But Khamira.

She lifts her head and sees that she has curled into a ball. She still has one hand on the wall, but she is looking into space with blood on her hands and her face. Zion shakes her head and decides to take who she can out of here. She already feels the loss for Kateri. And now Michael.

The boats are about 5 yards away from his body, so she is determined to take it with them.

"Khamira, I need your help. We are going to bring him into the boats." She implores Khamira to move and come towards her, but she isn't responding at all.

Zion hooks her arms beneath Michael's shoulders to prepare to drag him over to their escape route. She knows their time is short, and they still must eliminate the other boats. She pulls with all her might but feels soreness pulling in her back, and her left hip feels bruised. Still, she doesn't give up. "Please, God! Don't make me lose anyone else here!" She screams as she heaves again. "Please."

She waits a moment to catch her breath and fights the urge to crawl next to her younger counterpart.

"Kami!" She begs and sees a finch, but she still doesn't move.

"She prefers Khamira."

Her eyes snap to confused hazel orbs blinking at her. Blinking. "Michael?"

"Unless you're a friend." He finishes.

He's alive? He groans and goes to move. "He's alive!"

****

"I am very disappointed in you." He starts off like a parent simply telling his child he will be on time out. But Paul knows better. "We have nothing! No new information on the Adherens and nothing out of that God-forsaken Noble! You were spoken very highly of by all of my officials and captains. Nearly everyone vouched for you."

Paul looks Samael in the face as he rants but says nothing.

"I see that you have not been taking heed to my instruction. You have *yet* to accept the Portentum change. Do you insist on rebelling against everything I say?"

Paul remains silent.

"I believe that there needs to be an incentive for obedience. You see, if you give everyone true freedom, it will lead to rebellion. And that is the problem!" He says in epiphany.

This is the first time that Paul has been graced with the General Elect's presence in person, which means that there must be something that he is very worried about. Paul knows how these meetings go. Will this man be the last thing that he ever sees?

"Will you kill me now?" he asks straight to the point.

Abigor laughs. "Of course not. I am a leader who represents love and autonomy. Why would I kill you?"

Right. Love and autonomy. Unless you disagree with the General Elect, then you're the next missing person's case.

He gestures, and the door behind Paul opens, though he doesn't move until prompted.

"Is this your flock?"

Paul looks into the faces of all of them, young and old. His youngest charge winks and smiles when he makes eye contact with him. Gabriel. Paul fights the urge to roll his eyes. He obviously can't tell that this is *not* a room you want to be in.

He nods to Abigor, ignoring his slight against their names.

"Now, *these* men and women were trained well! They follow orders and somehow manage to have a brain as well. My own shadow guard can take notes from them. Perhaps they are simply in need of a new command? Huh?"

Paul bites his tongue. He picked this team himself and trained them. He knows that they're good. They're the best. He doesn't need the General Elect to tell him that.

"They do what it takes to complete our mission."

Here are all of the men and women that Paul has been working with for the past five years and now they stand with the general's shadow guard between them. It will be hard to be stripped of his leadership, but maybe they can still be on a team together.

He is also unsure of what information the team may have shared. Or what they could have agreed to. He hasn't seen them since they failed to catch Freeman.

"I am just and merciful. So, your incentive will lie with your men." Abigor says as if he is only now coming to a decision. "Yes, I am afraid that you need a little push." He points a finger out, and Paul follows it to see that he is singling out Gabriel and gesturing him forward. Paul tenses as he reaches his side. Now, Gabriel stands beside him and faces their leader. "Do you trust your commander?"

"Yes, General." He says with a confused glance at Paul.

"Do you trust him with your life?"

"Yes, General."

"And the rest of you agree?"

"Yes, General." They chorus and Paul are filled with pride in his team and himself.

"Good."

Each shadow guard pushes a button, and necklaces that once held identification tags collapse into a thin line, searing everything in its path like a cheese slicer or meat cleaver.

They fall to the ground one after another.

Paul roars, enraged, as he looks around in horror. He doesn't think about the smile on Abigor's face as he finally gives him the reaction he wanted. His men's bodies are dumped before him without care.

"Mercy?" His jaws ache at how tightly clenched they are.

"Of course." He sees the leader's eyes flick to his side, and Gabriel is gasping for breath and shaking after emptying his stomach. But he is alive.

Paul grabs him by the back of his neck and aids him to stand in one swift motion. Their left hands clasp each other's arms as if in a friendly shake, but both hold on like a lifeline.

Paul tries to tell him with his eyes that he is here. And that has to be enough.

But not for their leader.

"You, Paul Fenty, no children, estranged from your family. But you do have a sister. Faithful to the cause, I must say. If the Ravens weren't enough, I can do you one better. I know where your sister is. And I would hate for her to have to join your... birds." He doesn't wait for a response but gestures them out. He has done what he came to do. Paul takes in his people's faces, frozen in shock and pain. He drags Gabe from the room. He won't be another Raven who never got the chance to fly.

Chapter 21

"We've got a problem," Zion cringes. *That's not the first thing you want to hear after survival of the fittest.*

"No, thank you. We've got enough problems." She responds to Chaz. Khamira has been in a trance since Zion literally dragged her to the boat, and she is supporting half of Michael's weight. As soon as they enter the new location where the boats deposited them, she wants to drop everything and pass out, preferably for at least 48 hours. It's both comforting and scary to know that she is back in the bridge where all of this started. It seems so long ago.

"Ha ha." Chaz deadpans, but her calculating dark eyes take in their crew with a frown.

"Where is Kateri?" David asks from where he is huddled up with two older teens a boy and a girl and an older Nigerian man of medium height who she remembers is called Oji.

They all look curious for an answer. Michael tenses and Zion looks at the floor.

"She's dead." Khamira voices and Zion's gaze snaps to her, shocked. She has been nearly catatonic this whole time. But she frowns, realizing that Khamira just stated facts, her brain refusing to stop even in her grief. "She's dead and I... It's my fault." If it weren't for that one hitch in her sentence, you would think she is reading a newsletter. After she has said her piece, she walks to a curtained area that looks to house a pantry and no one stops her.

Zion pleads with her eyes for someone to change the subject, which, surprisingly, Chaz does.

"It's too bad girl genius is in a fit because we'll need help." Zion walks Michael over to a bench (it's actually the same one that she once relaxed on) and he nods in thanks.

The room looks dusty and smells dank like it's been unused, but it's pretty similar to the Hill headquarters. Except it is more like a bunker. A long mirror separates the two doors, and curtains cover many areas instead of actual doors.

"We'll have to manage on our own for now. We won't force Khamira to do anything more." Zion is unsure how Michael can still sound composed with a potentially broken ankle, a bruised face, and a bloody shirt. Thankfully, most of his injuries were superficial. But he looks like someone who needs a nurse, not command. "What's going on?"

"This." Ravi turns on the screen, and immediately, the room is overwhelmed with screams, terror, and chaos. The sound of guns and the red-orange of fire blend with black smoke in the atmosphere, creating a daunting nightmare.

"Oh my...." Zion fades as she realizes, "That's where Adri is!" The angle has changed, but the sign on the building with the tree and an apple has a chip in the exact same place.

The 11 guards have multiplied and are targeting the people who are running. But others are firing back. This crew of men and women with microfiber scarves covering the bottom of their faces are fighting.

"That moron, Jonathan, attacked the camp," Chaz explains. The screen shows women and men running but being shot down by both sides if caught in the crossfire. From the camera's view, the Allies seem to target the people running.

Each has scarves like those that Kateri and Michael wore when Zion was lightheaded in the Hill. The two groups seem so similar but they are very different!

There is a moment of peace as the shadow guards reload as one and Jonathan, the only unmasked person, starts a speech to his viewers. It's like he planned the violence just for this.

"Our leaders are murderers and liars! And the people of The Alliance are no fools. We will no longer accept this tyranny!" He steps forward, but the guards are no longer shooting. *Why?*

"This prison was created for those who disagree with the leaders. Do not allow yourselves to be blinded. Come! And ally with me, and you will have your way of escape. To be free to be yourself! If you conform, you will be made into a clone. Non-thinking sheep ready to be herded in whichever direction that you are steered. We will not stop until we are free!" He drops his arms to his side, and bright lights surround him in a circle that expands until it flashes to the cameras. When the light dims, they are gone.

But their destruction remains.

Everyone sits in silence and stares at the screens, surveying the damage. It's obviously intended to make the people question his methods and, in turn, his words.

"Was—did... are we the only ones who saw that?" Zion stammers with her hand over her mouth.

"No," Ravi says, "it was aired. Everyone saw it."

Michael places his hand over his head. "He's out of control!"

"He challenged the leaders on a platform." Chaz sounds impressed. "At least he's doing something besides sitting around waiting to be killed!"

"The problem is that the leaders will retaliate, and more people will die," Ravi says. "They are going to target that camp just to get to him."

"What! We've got to stop them!" Zion exclaims.

"How do you suggest we do that?" Oji asks in a thick Nigerian accent.

"I... I don't know. But we can't let those people die in the crossfire of some fight they aren't even aware of. We know where they are; we can get inside somehow and sneak them out!"

"You want to risk all of our lives just to save your friend?" Ravi asks. Not rudely, but Zion is defensive.

"There's gotta be a way to help my friend *and* everyone else there."

No one says anything. They won't even make eye contact, and she feels her anger stir.

"Will you all just do nothing? You're so worried about saving yourselves that you will hide away, and what? Wait for a new world order? None of you would even care about the camp if your people weren't there. You're selfish, all of you!"

"You have to understand—"

"You know what I understand, Ravi? You condemn Johnathan and Abigor and anyone who doesn't think like you. But you are the same. Careless about anyone else as long as your agenda continues, right?"

"Zion—"

"No!" She interrupts whatever excuse Michael is preparing. "'You don't have to lean into your fear. But you've got to have a little faith,' pretty words. Good to know that they mean nothing to you."

She dramatically turns away from them and begins walking towards the two doors. They call after her, but she doesn't pause even though she has no idea where she's going. She has to get away from these hypocrites. They preach love and freedom but only when it's convenient.

Turns out that the door that she rips open (the right one) leads to an open-concept room with eight bunk beds along the walls. There are a couple of brown doors, which may be bathrooms.

She paces the room a couple of times before flouncing onto one of the beds with her head in her hands.

The door clicks, and she doesn't look up to see who came after her.

"Hey, darling," Michael says. She glances at him and he is holding his side and leaning against the doorway. The sight almost causes her to feel guilty for making him come after her. Almost.

"You should skip the pep talk and get to bed." He looks exhausted.

"No can do. I drew the short straw for motivational speaking."

She bites her lip to smother a smile at his attempt at a joke.

"I'm going to find a way to get them out. I've already decided, so don't try to change my mind. You'd be wasting your breath and it doesn't look like you can afford to do that right now."

He chuckles and then grimaces. "You're probably right. Do you really care if I'm wasting my valuable breath?"

"At this moment, no." She lies.

He laughs and then grimaces again, making Zion wince in regret. Michael limps over to the nearest chair (bean bag) and lets out a frustrated groan.

"I just need a minute to... process. I— we— just lost Kateri, and now...I don't know... my mom is gone."

Zion's heart breaks, and she chides herself for being selfish and inconsiderate. *The mirror spares no flaws.*

"I know we need leadership. I know we should create a plan, but just... stay. Give me time. I don't want to watch you die."

The unspoken "too" is heard loud and clear.

Zion shrinks into herself, wishing she could hide from her feelings of shame. "I'm sorry." It isn't enough to take back her accusations or to try to empathize with his grief, especially when she cannot describe her own.

Time. She tells herself she can give him that, but she isn't sure everyone else can wait...

* * * * * * * * *

"Khamira. This is the last time I will ask you before I pull out you by your little afro."

And Chaz has lost it.

"Get up!"

"Chaz, we really shouldn't push." Zion intercedes. Again. "We do need you, though, Khamira."

"You're sad. We get it. But we're all sad, and we're going to *die* sad if you don't kick it into gear!" Chaz screams once again and gets no response.

It's been about 8 hours, and the most they have been able to do is get her into the room, which has only led to her curling up on one of the bunk beds.

After showering and sleeping, the big three — Michael, Chaz, and Ravi— finally agreed. But the plan hinges a lot on Khamira. No one else stands a chance against the tech on the other side. There has been silence from Jonathan and the shadow guards since *the incident,* which has put everyone on edge. No one knows what's going on in the camp, and the networks have been useless, only describing the damage done by the Allies.

No one seems to want to make a move which is why the Adherens want to strike now before they decide to. And this is where Chaz wants Khamira to come in.

"Stop yelling at her, Charlotte." Ravi drones. *Charlotte*? "She is only a kid." Chaz rolls her eyes, and he rubs her back affectionately.

Okay, what is happening there?

"No one cares that she's only 15 any other time. She's smart and mature and, therefore, accountable. There's no place for children. We've all lost our childhood."

Fifteen. Zion was eighteen when she lost her last living relative. Her grandmother Dollie.

"Can I speak to her alone?" She asks the pair. Michael is still recovering from his trauma and hasn't woken up even from Chaz's yelling.

All the others are in a garden through the left door. Ravi nods to her and takes a grumbling Chaz to join them.

When Zion is alone with Khamira, she takes her hand on the bed. "Come with me, love."

The young girl doesn't look her in the eyes but doesn't fight when she brings her to a stool in one of the two restrooms. While everyone was resting, Zion found some time for self-care.

She grabs the supplies that she found. With a bottle warmer, she warms a towel and wrings it. She uses it to wipe Khamira's face, taking care with her eyes, and then she repeats the process and wipes her hands off. Brown eyes meet, and Zion sees her charge, staring at her as if she's never seen her before, like a newly discovered creature. Yet she is silent.

Zion begins to hum as she takes a jar with flaxseed gel and rosemary leaves to detangle her hair. She uses her fingers on small sections, nurturing each strand. She coils her hair with the gel, making her curls even more defined.

Time passes with only her humming, breaking the silence, and Khamira has closed her eyes, but tears run down her face, dripping onto her clasped hands.

Zion sees her tears, but she keeps humming and working through until the back of her hair is complete. Khamira's tears still flow, and Zion finally speaks.

"I know you want to shut down. I can't imagine how you feel or what you are going through. But grief and depression are like leeches. They will suck the life out of you until you have nothing left. I didn't get to know Kateri that well, but I know she would not blame you, and you shouldn't blame yourself. Khamira, I am a teacher and have seen a lot of smart students, but never anyone as gifted as you. The way you see the world... I can't even begin to comprehend!"

She says nothing.

Zion takes more of her homemade hair products and continues with her wash and go.

"I— I made that bomb!" Khamira starts sobbing in earnest. "She told me not to, and I did it anyway. She died because I couldn't just listen!"

Zion pauses before continuing her self-made task.

"We all would have died or been captured if Kateri hadn't made that sacrifice. Don't minimize that." She lightly chastises, not wanting her to close back up. "You have helped so many people, including me." she walks around to meet her eyes, "the night goggles, the shoe covers, the map! Everything. Ravi told me that you made all that stuff, and I never said it, but thank you." Zion crouches in front of her. "Even something painful can have a purpose."

"I didn't make that stuff alone. My sister... she left. My mom, Kateri! Why does everyone leave me?" Zion realizes that she doesn't show it the same, but she has insecurities and feelings that get overlooked because of her intelligence.

She wraps her arms around her. "I don't know why your sister left, but the way you have wormed your way into my heart, I would do anything I could to keep you safe. Even if that meant we had to be separate for a while." Her voice cracks, thinking of her own sister's sacrifice for her to get to safety.

"How do you do it?"

"Do what?"

"Mess up all the time? How does it not destroy you?" Zion pauses. Khamira's blunt nature, as usual, catches her off guard.

"I just know I'm not perfect, so I focus on what I *can* do. I let go of the rest."

"It must be very overwhelming to make mistakes all the time." Zion bites her lip to hide a chuckle. *She's trying to comfort me!*

"Yes, Jesus loves me."

"What?" Now, she's just confused.

"That's what you were humming."

It was the song that her grandmother hummed while doing ponytails and twists in Zion's own hair.

"Do you believe that?" Zion asks, curious, unsure if Khamira's neurodivergent nature will lead her away from God.

A pause. *Is that too personal?* Zion starts panicking, thinking she pushed the already overwhelmed teen too far.

"I don't express emotions very well. Powerful ones especially. But I feel a lot. I do believe it." She places her hand on her chest. "I feel it."

"You feel God? How do you know that's what it is?"

"God fills in the space. I'm smart and can create and understand a lot, but there is space." She looks intently at the older woman as if she wants to force understanding on Zion, and it makes her smile.

"And God fills the spaces where you don't understand?"

"No. God makes the spaces work."

Zion thinks about the simple explanation.

"Do you get it?"

For the first time in her life, "I'm starting to."

"Zion?"

"Yeah?"

"You can call me Kami."

Chapter 22

*W*ar.

That's what Paul thinks as he surveys the terrain of bodies flowering the camp. This is his second visit in two days, and his purposes couldn't be more different. *It's not only me that has changed,* he thinks as he looks around.

Before, people littered the courtyard. Now, everyone is confined to their rooms or cells, depending on which side of the bars you're on.

After the Allies, as they've dubbed themselves, attacked, the violence for rebellion became even more widespread.

People everywhere are being detained and even killed for misdemeanors. His new sect, he grimaces, is cruel and all marked with the *Portentum Change*.

He's running out of time.

Paul flashes his *Vistigeum* at the gates and braces, unsure if they will still open. They do and he exhales. *That's a relief.*

The shadow guards follow his movement down the hall, each turning their heads one by one until he is out of their sight. Paul forces himself not to move faster, but it seems like he can hear the ticking of an internal clock signaling him as he walks.

He sees the faces of his men. People that he was tasked to lead and protect, and now... he shakes his head. *Focus on who you can save.*

When he reaches the stone door he is looking for, he pauses. No turning back now.

He rips open the door and connects the interference device that he was given, which will block all surveillance of this conversation.

"I need to know if you have contact with the Allies."

He freezes

In his haste, Paul ignored the first rule of Recon: Assess the situation.

His eyes fully adjust to the darkness, and where he expected to face suspicious brown eyes refusing to answer questions; instead, he sees those eyes pleading and full of fear.

Adria faces him with a hand around her neck and a weapon pointed toward her head. He doesn't remember taking out his blaster but finds it in his hands by instinct.

"Yeah. Some may say that I have *frequent* contact with the Allies." His opponent chuckles. Paul recognizes him; how could he not when he just named himself public enemy number one?

Paul doesn't respond. How likely is it that they all leave the room alive?

"I'd say that the name inspires confidence, don't you think love?" he asks Adria, forcing her face closer in a way that would be intimate but for the deadly appendage pushed against her skull.

 "She doesn't seem to think so," Paul answers. "Why don't you let her go, and you and I talk."

He shrugs, "She'll come around, and besides, *she's* not in any danger from me. You, on the other hand, well, that depends."

"On?"

"What do you want to see the Allies for?"

"I have questions."

He tenses, causing Adria to whimper, and his grip loosens. *That's curious.*

"I don't answer questions. You can go."

"Jonathan..." Adria pleads. Her eyes flit to Paul. He can't name the emotion he sees, but he will not abandon her.

"Let her go," Paul commands, standing to his full height and shifting his weight more threateningly. "Or I may not be as friendly."

He laughs boisterously. "We wouldn't want that." His response is dripping with sarcasm. "It doesn't matter anyway."

Paul furrows his brows.

"Johnathan..." She warns.

"Sorry, love."

Boom!

* * * * * * * * *

"We're here. Does everyone know the objective?" Ravi's drawling voice carries through the mics each member of the small group wear behind their ear.

"Yeah, yeah," Khamira inserts impatiently, "get as many people out as possible. And make sure no one dies."

"Yes, thank you for that summary, Khamira." Ravi continues. "This is a simple mission: get in and out. And *stay with your partner*."

Three pairs are wearing hideous, matching grey jumpsuits with different tasks to accomplish. Chaz and Oji (who looks like he has seen war many times before) will go into what should be the armory since they have the most battle experience. They are getting equipment and supplies.

Ravi and Khamira are going to the probable location of the intelligence center with a lot of reluctance from the latter (*"I'm much better behind a screen"*). These two are going to open the doors and release as many people as possible while locating high priority people of interest in and out of the camp.

Zion is with a curly-haired boy who looks like he is just out of his teens. They're paired together but she can't seem to remember his name but, it would be awkward to ask now. They are meant to find Adria and get back to the Bridge as soon as possible.

239

Michael stayed behind because, despite what he thinks, he can't contribute anything in his state.

"Each map is downloaded on your glasses. So, if you get lost or die, it's not my fault." Khamira adds. "And we should make sure that at least one of us returns to feed David."

Great pep talk.

"Let's go," Ravi says, as he is technically in charge.

Zion clicks on her glasses and sees the familiar lines and lights to guide her.

"It's Zion, right?" she hears from behind her before she gets too far.

She hmms.

And there is silence, so she stops and turns to face him. *What is his name again?*

"I guess I'm with you, huh?" He continues.

"Yep." *Obviously...*

"That's cool. I haven't had the chance to get to know you."

"Oh… umm, is now a good time for that?" She tries to ask as kindly as possible. *And what is his name? John? James? Chris? Something like that.*

"No, no, you're right. I'm just nervous." She nods as her own anxiety resurfaces. They need to get in and out, one foot in front of the other.

They start quickly walking from the South entrance into the tunnels. Each two-person team had different ejection spots. Zion and her partner – *Thomas?* — are going to the place where, if Khamira's calculations can be trusted —*she will kill me for asking that*— the most likely place for Adria would be.

All the teams should be on the lookout to find Noble, and should they find her, they are to report to Michael as soon as possible. No one seems to think that that will happen though. Not without inside help.

Besides that, there is no communication until each team is out of the camp's territory. Kami said something about it giving them away.

Michael seems certain that Noble won't be killed and is adamant that her help would be invaluable, but who knows what could have happened to her. What could happen to all of them. How the heck are they supposed to *survive* past tomorrow?

Zion shakes her head and refocuses. Think about today, today and worry about tomorrow, tomorrow.

She and her partner walk together in silence slowly, and it feels like they are alone.

"Are you scared?" The boy— Warren, maybe? — asks but doesn't seem to need a response. "It's been months since I've been out of the Hill. It just feels so safe there. Well, it *felt* that way. You weren't there long, but it... It's a family, you know?"

"Try to relax." His nerves are making her nervous. Obviously, neither of them is very experienced, and Ravi wanted them together since they are the least likely to see action. The thing about odds is that there is always a chance.

Boom!

Dust falls around the pair, and they struggle to hold their ground. Zion crouches down, not knowing where the attack is coming from, but sees the kid standing and frantically looking back and forth.

"Get down, kid!"

The two wait until the dust settles, and they cautiously stand.

"What was that?" He whispers.

"I—"

"What was that!" He panics.

"I don't know, but we have to hurry and get Adri and the others before it happens again."

He grabs her arm to stop her. "We should go back! Like right now!"

"No!" She pulls her arm away and creates distance between them. "You can go if you want, but I'm not leaving, Christian!"

He pauses in confusion. "I—my name is Chase."

Zion flushes but does not back down. "Are you leaving?"

He looks down in shame, "I just turned 18. I don't want to die." Zion is disappointed, but she nods and turns around.

"I understand… Chase." She figures that she should call him by his real name at least once. "You should go."

"But—"

"I'm not leaving. I can't go back with her." She waits for his response, but she only hears his steps begin to lead away and eventually fade to nothingness. When she can no longer hear him, she turns around. *Maybe I should go back.* She is unsure about the blast and feels her anxiety threatening to take hold. "But I'm so close." She hesitates, holding onto her calm by a thread, and then adds, "God...She is all I have, and please help me do this."

She knows that it's hypocritical. To call on a God that she has doubts about, but she feels desperation as she is once again in an impossible situation.

Zion eases forward, taking notice of the steel bars on either side of her, and hopes that this isn't what she will need to overcome for her sister.

The quiet seems to scream...

"No!"

That's a real scream. And one that she knows.

Adria! Her chocolate orbs widen, and she sprints down the long hall. Her steps echo, making her ears pound. She keeps moving, grateful that there aren't too many branches from the main path.

The steel blends together as she runs, and she passes the shock of two men fighting in an open room. She backtracks until she takes in the scene before her quietly.

There are two men in a fight for dominance, with an inconspicuous Adria creeping up behind them, and neither notices the weapon in her hand.

But who's the target?

Jonathan is here— of course he is— and the officer... Paul, she remembers. Zion can never understand the bond between Jonathan and Adria. The two are opposites yet always seem to be drawn together. He is like a flame to her moth. But how close can you get before you are burnt?

It looks like she is planning to stop the two, and Zion is ignored as she shakes her head for her to stay out of it.

Adria raises her arm high and swings down to strike... Jonathan?

He looks shocked more than hurt.

What is going on?

"Adria?" Jonathan asks, hurt.

Adria flinches as if she struck herself.

Paul finishes off a distracted Jonathan with a strike to the temple, effectively neutralizing that threat for now.

"I'm confused." Zion voices, and she barely has a moment to brace before she is wrapped in the arms of her sister.

"Are you okay—"

"I was so worried—"

They both speak at the same time and Adri squeals and goes for another hug at the familiarity of the scene.

"I wasn't sure since we were..."

"Haven't spoken since we were separated." Adria interrupts her with a pointed look at their company. Unfortunately, Zion isn't the only one who notices.

"Another crisis that I find you at the center of," Paul says, changing the atmosphere from one of sisterhood to weariness like that of an animal determining whether the man before her is a hunter or friend.

"I wouldn't say the center," Zion whispers softly.

"You didn't waste any time with your new friends. Remember what I said?"

"You made friends?" Adria's excited question is ignored.

"I told you that I didn't want to find out that you have hurt one person—"

"I haven't!"

"And yet, here you are. After your Allies have murdered innocent people."

"They aren't *my* Allies! And besides, why are all of these people here if you think they are innocent?" Zion defends.

Paul pauses and sighs. "I've gotten a lot of information about the Adherens and the Allies from a very reliable source." He takes in both young women before him. "I think we should talk."

* * * * * * * * *

"Where are we?" Adria asks Paul, who has revealed a door from the hall that they just turned off. The three of them and an unconscious Jonathan, who is being dragged on some type of blanket, are so far underground that Zion worries Khamira's technology won't be able to locate her if she finds trouble.

"This is the key. Now, we only need to join the race opening the door."

"Why a riddle?" she complains, and his lips upturn as he pushes the door in.

There is a very bare room with a single twin-sized cot, a toilet, and a desk, all connected to the wall and the floor. Paul drags Johnny over and drops him unceremoniously near the desk.

"Hey!" Adria goes over to check on him as Paul cuffs him to the base. "You can be more gentle."

"You struck him." She looks away, guilty. "We should have a talk about your choice in men."

Zion takes in the dark room, trying not to look at her sister with I-told-you-so eyes. This place is a steel box. Whatever is here is super secure. "What is this place?" She can't help but whisper as if speaking louder will incite the evil to attack her.

"Welcome back, Mr. Fenty." Zion's head whips in the direction of the furthest corner, where she can just make out a silhouette of a woman. *How did I not see her?* "And with company. I'd welcome you, but I'm afraid I'm not quite up to it." She steps into view, and Zion is finally able to put a face to a voice and a name.

"You'd better get up to it because you are very popular." He looks her over for any injuries. Her voice is familiar...

"LaQuinn Noble?" she asks with wide eyes.

She smirks and is a mirror image of... Khamira when she feels like she is the smartest in the room (which is all the time). Now, looking over her with new eyes, she can see her young friend in Ms. Noble's face. The almond-shaped eyes and full lips. She has a head full of thick waist-length sister locks with red scabs along her hairline.

"At your service. It's nice to meet a fellow troublemaker. I hear that you have been causing quite the stir with the New Order of The World Alliance."

"So... What does this creepy place have to do with a key?" Adria questions, leaving her space from Johnathan's side to join the others.

"The key?" Noble seems amused by the description.

"It's not this place, Adri, it's her."

"Very good you!" She praises, and Zion blushes. She is reminded of herself teaching third graders.

"You remind me of your daughter." Sadness takes over Noble's face.

"Elisha? You've seen her?"

"No... sorry. You just reminded me of a young girl I met a bit ago."

She smiles sadly. "Khamira."

"Yeah. She helped me get here. She is really amazing. Is she your daughter?"

"Yes, she is, but I was not much of a mother to her or my older daughter. "She is unsure of how to answer but is saved when she continues.

"Is she well?"

"Yes." Zion feels that she can trust everyone in this room — except Jonathan — even though Paul threatens her each time they meet. "She is now."

She nods, and Zion wants to ask for the rest of the story, but she doesn't and Noble nods to her like she is grateful.

"Not to interrupt," Adria interrupts, "But why is she the key?"

No one answers. Zion is unsure of what to say as she knows that everyone wants the scientist but not the why.

"Because. I created the *vistigeum*. And I spearheaded the *Portentum Change*, which is near the top of my list of transgressions, but not the worst that I have done." Noble shakes her head in shame and turns away from them. "I was overconfident in my own genius. My own ability. I knew the danger, but I created a formula. Following the pathway to nerves in the brain and everything that makes us human. I developed a way to disengage the ventromedial prefrontal cortex, and interestingly enough, you can choose where the signal engages. In what it disengages. With the *Change,* there is a signal that interrupts a person's connection with faith."

"But wouldn't that change us from what makes us who we are?" Adria asks.

"No. This would only be aimed toward one connection to our most spiritual selves."

"Belief?" Paul suggests, but Zion has realized the big picture. They want to disconnect everyone from...

"God."

Chapter 23

In the times since the creation of The World Alliance, there has been teachings that God is a way for your brain to deal with trauma and misunderstanding. A figment that the brain creates. Imagination. People create their own destinies and their own future. Their own gods.

But this... What they just heard is proof that all of it was a lie. It's one thing to have faith that what you believe is true and another to have proof. Why try to use this weapon if there was not a real deity?

"Anyone who accepts the *change* will have it activated. Wherever and whenever the leader chooses. Once it's implanted, it can't be detached. It's called the Expungement Project. A dear friend helped me to see the error of my ways. His name was Jameson De Leon. He became close with Elisha, my oldest daughter, just before she disappeared."

"But doesn't that mean that people can be forced into it?" Zion asks, not missing the past tense used when speaking of her friend.

Noble is already shaking her head, "In our trials, forcefully implanted microchips always lead to corrosive chips and death. It won't latch if it is not voluntary. Even when the neurotransmitters are released slowly into the nervous system, the rejection has been 100% if not taken willingly. It's similar to a body rejecting an organ except that it is much more rapid." She explains.

"It's like the sediment that broke my bracelet."

"*Sentience.* And it is exactly like that but becoming a part of you. And instead of preventing toxins, it would release them. All of us who have taken the *change* will not be able to prevent the altering of DNA unless we were to die before the activation."

"All of us?" Zion sees that she does not have a bracelet on, and between her thumb and forefinger is a mark with an upside-down triangle with lines that start from each angle and look like the letter Y with a curving tail. This is the first time that she has seen a mark of *change* up close, and she shivers. "You accepted the *change*?"

"I have. I was one of the first. You must understand this *change* was meant to be a good thing. It is a way to monitor for internal diseases, detect mental illness, determine hereditary disorders, and more than health. It could provide a better financial security system and ensure that everyone has apt resources. There could even be national security. Imagine a world with no war! Of course, I was glad to partake in my own design." She said, and Zion sees Paul checking a watch of some sort. Better make this quick, then.

"So, what happened? What made you change your mind?" She asks.

"My daughter. The oldest. She saw what I was doing and started to experiment with the *Sentience* and the *Portentum Change*. She became different, seeing things and hallucinating. She is the most intelligent and beautiful person that I have ever seen, not just because I am her mother. She cared more about others, especially her sister, than science, so she used herself as a subject. And it drove her to insanity. Once I realized the danger, I sent Khamira away. Now I am caught up in the race."

"Why is there a race?" Adria asks, "It sounds like it's already done, and everyone who has accepted *change* is a goner." Noble smiles.

"Elisha created a core before she disappeared. A way to prevent neurotransmitters from being dispatched. I replicated it for all who made a mistake."

"A do-over," Zion whispers.

"It can be initiated as long as the change is not complete."

"Now that," all eyes snap to the very awake chained man grinning like he has a winning lottery ticket in hand. "That sounds like something I may be interested in."

Paul pulls out his weapon.

"Too late, Captain." He bites down hard on something between his teeth, and a series of quakes shake them from their feet. Debris falls, and there is a feminine yell. Zion looks over at Jonathan who is still attached to the table, but he does not look concerned with being buried alive like the rest of them.

He watches them all struggle, and his lips are moving, but she can't quite make out what he is saying. She crawls nearer through another shake, and she hears him mumbling.

"… rook takes bishop, knight takes rook, and check." He makes eye contact with her and tilts his head. "What's your move?"

Is this a game to him? She shakes her head and jumps at a hand on her shoulder.

"Jonathan, stop this!"

"Don't you see Adria! This is the solution for all of us! Do you know what we can do with this? We can make everyone change their minds about following the agenda! All the changes that the leaders have made will have been for nothing! We will be free once more." He laughs boisterously through the noise around them.

Zion wishes for a distress signal now more than ever. She notes that Paul has moved in front of Noble. She has no idea how this will all end.

"John..." Adri sounds disappointed. He finally pauses. She stands tall (as best she can) and continues, "If you do that, manipulate people for your benefit, you'll be doing the same thing as the people you hate. What happened to you, Jonathan?"

"What happened?" He says derisively, "My family has been chased down and killed for an agenda. I've had to give up everything! Even you! If I have to be like the leaders to beat them, then I will."

Zion can understand, and she even sees a glimpse of the real him in this moment. If only they could work with *this* version of him instead of the douchebag that he usually is, then they would have a lot more success in… Wait!

"Call off the attack!" She yells out suddenly, and Johnathan's eyes cut to her with derision. "We can help each other. I— I have an idea." Only the sound of the ground rumbling is heard in consistent waves. Jonathan's eyes go between the two pairs. Paul is in front of a kneeling Noble with his weapon still leveled at him and the two sisters are holding each other up. He looks at Adria for a second longer, and then he rolls his eyes away.

"There is a remote on my neck. It'll stop the shocks." Adri heads over as fast as she is able and grabs the remote. The two make eye contact, and her finger hovers over the single button. "Trust me."

Nope.

But apparently, her sister does because she presses down, and the shaking gradually slows and then settles. She beams at him, and he gives a crooked smile in return.

"Unfortunately, it doesn't stop the attack." He says to her, and she pulls back.

"What do you mean?"

"The signal is out. The camp is coming down. 10 minutes, maybe 15."

"What!"

He shrugs.

"Thanks," Paul says to him, straightening out. "You just made this job a whole lot harder. Unfortunately, the fireworks move up our timeline." Paul looks at his watch again before turning to Noble, "How would you like to get out of here?"

She smiles, which gives her a mystical look. "I could do a change of scenery. And besides, I think that with my talented daughter at my side, we can figure out a way to save a lot of people."

"What exactly is the Allies plan, Johnathan?"

"The Allies! It has a ring to it, right?" He is faced with unamused faces and he rolls his eyes. "Sheesh... Tough crowd. We've been smuggling people out since yesterday. The camp should be mostly empty now."

"You didn't seem to care about people's lives when you were shooting them down with your temper tantrum." Paul snarks, heading for the door.

"That wasn't what it looked like. Really! The leaders made sure we looked like killers and crazy people when the shadow guards were the ones uncaring for people's lives. We may not agree on everything, but we protect the innocent."

Paul huffs.

"And am I to go down with the ship?" Jonathan asks, still cuffed.

"You caused it to go down." Paul retorts.

"Are you going to just leave him here? He'll be killed." Adria adds.

"What do you suggest? Now that he's decided not to be a villain." Paul asks sarcastically.

"He can come with us." Zion moves to stop Paul's stride. "He can give us the resources to make Ms. Noble's plan, whatever it is, a reality."

"Fine," Paul says, looking directly at her, "a word?" That sounds foreboding. He hands a key to Noble and directs them down the hall to the left. After a minute, it is only the two of them.

She tries not to fidget under his scrutiny, but she can't help tugging on her hair. Today, she went with a deep part and two flat twists, which curved like a crown into a plait at the back of her head. She wishes that the gray jumpsuit had pockets or buttons or something for her to mess with, but besides the goggles that rest on her head, the shoe covers, and a watch, she has nothing extra. She feels bare and vulnerable under his gaze.

"You have made friends with the wrong group." *Is he worried?* "You should take your 'sister' and run."

"My friends have kept me sane through all of this. They aren't perfect, but they are exactly what I needed. Besides, if we run, we both know that we'd be dead within a day."

"I know a place. And the stray that you just picked up; he is going to get you killed."

"I know how to keep him in check. Besides, I am a good judge of character."

"Wrong."

"I knew I could trust *you*. You're on our side." That is apparently not the right thing to say. He steps into her personal space and points a finger to her chest.

"Ideas like that get you killed! They get everyone around you killed! Do you have any idea what's at stake?"

Her eyes are wide and show her emotions clear as day. Fear, anxiety, contempt, pride all wrestle for dominance in them.

He is not satisfied.

"Samael Abigor, our General Elect—"

"I know who he is."

"— wants *you* dead. And you can bet that he knows that you're here today."

"Why does he care so much about *me*?" She complains.

He scoffs in disbelief, "You don't know? Of course, you don't. Two days ago, right after your wanted notice came out, there were notices about you. About who you were, where you came from, that kind of thing. For 24 hours, there was propaganda about you, a normal school-teacher, saying no. Now, you are a symbol of rebellion."

"What!"

"The leaders have known about the Adherens, but it's much more fun to stamp out a flame when it's hot. He's playing all of the Adherens like puppets. And your 'friends' are using you. You just keep playing a losing hand."

"Uh! How am I supposed to play along when I don't know the game? I can't play my cards right because I don't have any cards!" Zion throws her hands up in frustration.

"It's not about the Adherens anymore. Some people are saying that you're a hero. Do you know what that means? Hundreds have risen all around the world in defiance. He's associating that with you. Vigilantes and people all over are using you as a reason to fight back. There's no way The General is going to let that go on, and the Adherens won't let it go."

"So, should I just hide? And let all of those people fight alone?"

"No. You should play a different game."

The two make eye contact. He was mad that she said she trusts him, but she knows that she can, and she still does. Play a different game. She takes a deep breath and closes her eyes.

"We need to go," Paul says.

"You said it yourself; everyone knows I'm here. Why not just get it over with and be captured?" She hears some rustling.

"Here." She opens her eyes and sees a stick of gum. "Now stop pitying yourself and dig out a rule book. I didn't tell you to stop playing. Just change the rules of the game." *Changing the rules makes it a different game.* A light comes on, and he sees. "Good. Now, keep going down this pathway until you see a red line on the bottom of the wall like this one. That door will take you toward where your trail *first* ran cold. It's a couple of miles around, but it'll get you out of here undetected."

"What will you do? If the leaders know about me, then they most likely know about you, too."

He smirks. "I'm going to keep doing my job and protect the peace. True peace."

"Paul." he hmms. "Thank you."

He waves it off, "Here," He hands her a jacket which she hasn't seen since... "Try to keep up with your things. And take care of yourself, Miss Freeman; look after Miss Stone. It'd be a shame for all this sacrifice to go to waste."

Chapter 24

Do you think I should contact them now?"

"I still can't believe that we got out of there in one piece!" Adria responds to Zion.

"I know." The team of four left through the exit and found a van with a destination locked in. They only encountered one guard who waved them through the front gates. Zion lifts her eyes to the sky in thought. Everything happened so perfectly, but she is still tense, waiting for the other shoe to drop.

"We are out of the prison's transmission zone." Ms. Noble adds from across the younger ladies.

"Great!" Johnathan claps and slides open the barrier between the back and the front. "Call up your pushover friends. I need to make a stop."

"What? Are you crazy, Johnny?"

"Just crazy enough, love." He laughs with a wink, and Zion fakes a gag.

"I definitely should have left him." Zion mumbles and reaches for her HEDY device. "Hello?" There is silence. What if something is wrong? She looks around the van, and everyone is waiting for a response. Where will they go if not to the Adherens? Definitely not to the Allies. But what choice do they have?

"Hello? Is anyone—"

"Zion!"

She sighs in relief. "Kami."

"It was really probable that you were dead or captured."

"Uh… right. Did everyone else make it back?"

"Yeah, everyone except you guys."

Zion smiles in relief "That's great."

"Ask for their location," Johnathan says without looking up from a now exposed panel with wires, buttons, and pads.

"We're at the bridge," Khamira answers. "Activate your goggles, and I can give you the directions to get you here."

She follows the order and pulls her goggles onto her face. She sees the visuals change, lines disappearing and changing to a new course. "Wow. It's really amazing to see this in real-time."

"I know."

And there goes that conversation, Zion chuckles. "I'm glad you're okay, Kami."

"Why aren't you following the guide?"

Paying closer attention, she can see that the van is traveling opposite the prompts on the goggles, causing them to constantly readjust. Johnathan.

"Where are we going?" She demands.

"We're almost there." He rolls his eyes.

"That's not an answer."

"That's all the answer you're going to get, teacher."

"How can you stand him?" She asks Adria, who shrugs her shoulders and goes over to him to whisper in smaller voices. Hopefully, to teach him how to be a human.

"We're taking a detour," she tells Khamira in her earpiece.

"That's not very intelligent." she hears in response.

Suddenly, the van stops. Jonathan flashes the occupants of the van a smile and then jumps out of their shield. There is silence for a moment.

"Did he...He wouldn't have set us up?"

"He wouldn't." Zion hears Adri's unspoken, "Would he?" All the women wait in silence for his return, and finally, he does with a shadow guard.

"I was a fool for ever trusting you." Zion scowls.

"Glad you finally see that." He smirks in response.

"You're really betraying us?" Adria whispers, hurt evident in her voice. He pauses, and the infernal smirk falls from his face. Finally, he speaks.

"Not yet."

At a nod to the shadow guard, the helmet is taken off.

"Aoife?" Adri recognizes.

"You remembered her name?" Zion whispers to her.

"I make it a point to remember the names of everyone who looks like they want to kill me."

"Happy?" Even though he doesn't look at anyone in particular, every person in the van knows who he is really asking.

"You could've just told us."

He scoffs and mumbles what sounds like "that's no fun."

"Well, this has been enlightening, but I would love to see my daughter." Noble reminds them of her presence.

"Yeah, yeah. Hand over your fancy glasses, teacher. We've got a show to see."

* * * * * * * * *

"Zion! There you are!"

Khamira's guide finally gets the small group joined with their main counterparts. The first people that they see are Ravi and Michael. The latter looks much better, but he is still guarding his ribs.

They are at the bridge where she first met him. Apparently, it connects to the bunker where they all were yesterday.

"We didn't know what to think when you guys didn't come back." Michael hugs her, and Ravi grabs her shoulder, making her feel more at home. His eyes scan the small group, and his face goes through many emotions before he settles on a frown.

"Where is Chase?"

"He— what? He went back almost as soon as we heard the first blast. I-I sent him on without me." She glances at Ravi and looks away. "I couldn't leave Adri."

She sees the accusation in his eyes even before he says anything. He told them to stay together.

"Wow." Everyone's favorite vigilante comments. "Already trouble in paradise? This is promising."

"Why is he here?" Michael says without making eye contact with him.

"He's going to help us."

"Absolutely not."

"We can get more done by working together."

"I agree," LaQuinn adds.

Michael spares her a quick smile. "Good to see you, Quinn." And the frown is back. "We've had our share of problems with the 'Allies'. They just killed and injured innocent people! We can't risk being associated with people like that."

"It wasn't what it looked like." He is ignored again.

"We have a one-strike rule. Anything fishy, and he's gone." Zion suggests looking at the subject of their conversation to see if he agrees.

"Yeah, yeah. But instead of trying to get rid of me, aren't you missing a man?"

"So, Chase isn't here?" Zion asks again.

"No."

Zion bites her lip in worry.

"Is there any way to find him? GPS?"

The boys sigh, and Ravi throws another suspicious glance at Johnathan before the two lead them in (much faster than Michael's first attempt with the stone wall). "Khamira will have the answers to those questions."

Noble visibly perks up at Kami's name.

As they move forward, Zion notices that they are approaching the bridge where she and Michael first met. It leads to the room that they've been bunking in.

Even though she feels like she is safe once again, she is anxious about where Chase is. She couldn't even remember his name, but now he is plaguing her thoughts.

****

"People of The World Alliance. I regret to inform you of another act of terror here on our land in our times of peace. Another attack took place and unfortunately resulted in 18 dead and eight shadow guards injured. The people who committed this crime follow a woman named Zion Freeman. Ironically, instead of representing a city of refuge, this woman and her allies, the Adherens, have brought destruction and evil. We must commit to The Change *in order to smoke out our enemies. We mourn our losses, but we do not give in to fear. Love is greater than pain. We shall look into the faces of our enemies and fight on. We will silence the voices of the city."*

****

How did it come to this in so few days? A week ago, she just wanted to teach her kiddos. She wanted to get away from war, and now she is at the center of it.

"Zion," Noble says softly, but she needn't have said anything. She can't look away from the small screen even though she wants nothing more than to do just that.

The speech was a cover to distract the masses from the truth. He won't just defame her, but he wants to destroy her.

"I know that you are listening to this." Even his voice is as slippery as a snake. She can't see his face, but he sounds satisfied like he knows that this blow hurts. *"Your little stunt at the camp was a nice touch. Rally the people, huh? Well, your time is short. Very short, in fact. It's too late for any changes to have a lasting impact, don't you see that?"*

"How is he doing this?" Michael asks, "Are we compromised?"

"He is sending a transmission. But he hasn't located us." Khamira answers with an iron grip on her mother's arm.

Yet.

"No matter. Dr. Noble, I hope you enjoy the time that you have left with your daughter. Yes, I know that you have joined them. But you have stopped nothing. Plans are still in motion, though I do wish to share some exciting news. Zion Freeman, you seem to have forgotten something. Not to worry, I will take care of it, as I will the rest of your interference."

Zion gasps, and she hears screams and yells of outrage all around her.

The kid—Chase— has his face frozen and fearful, but his eyes are lifeless. His body is not mangled, which is almost worse because the imagination of what could cause such an emotion to embody his last moments.

"Enjoy the last days of your freedom."

Everyone is silent as the image does not move. Khamira is pushing multiple keys, but the stillness remains.

There are sniffles and sobs, but no one says anything.

Zion can't stand to look at it another minute. She runs to the door, which she knows leads to the outdoors. She doesn't stop… she has to keep going. She runs as fast as she's able. She runs and doesn't look back because she knows that everything that she is running from is right behind her.

She can't escape. Her fears keep up with her, and if she stops, then they will attack her worse than before. Her fear, her pain, her loneliness.

Chapter 25

She thought she'd be better when Adria was here and when

Khamira started to open up. Michael, Ravi, Chaz, LaQuinn, Oji, and even little David have become like family. Isn't there a saying that says that nothing brings people together like tragedy?

But they don't get it! She's chasing... Something.

If she could spare her breath, she would laugh. It's funny how things change. Where she was running, now she's chasing. Every situation is like a word. The meaning can change with the slightest inflection, and the evening is now evening. Leveling out imperfections, imbalance, impotent, impractical, impossible!

Zion's body finally starts to slow, not fully able to keep up with her racing thoughts.

It's funny how you don't notice pain until attention is brought to it. The stitch in her side mocks her.

She sits to catch her breath and takes in her surroundings. She has no idea where she is, but it's quiet. So quiet that even the yelling in her brain short circuits for a glorious moment. There is nothing but a gentle breeze. It's almost as if it is a caress, like her grandmother's warm hands drying her face or lifting her head.

"I am all alone." Zion hears her own voice in a memory. She is a child again, asking her grandmother to take away her loneliness.

* * * * * * * * * *

"Close your eyes." She did, and there was darkness. Her grandmother said nothing else.

Young Zion felt even more alone than before.

She thought the older woman would help, but this was worse. She became impatient, so she peeked an eye open and... she truly left. Her mouth dropped open, and she looked around to see that she was now truly alone.

The one person who she knew wouldn't leave her did just that.

Her eyes watered, but before her first tear fell...

"I'm right here, lovely."

Following the voice, she saw the grays of her grandmother's hair framing her smiling face. She had taken a seat in her rocking chair, which faced away from where she stood, hiding herself away.

"Why did you leave me?"

"You silly girl," she cradled her face in her hands fondly, "I was here all the time. Just because you didn't see me doesn't mean I wasn't here. When you don't see God, and you don't feel him, and you can't track him. I am always there."

"You?" She asked, confused, "When I don't have God, you'll still be here?"

She felt silly as her elder lets out a melodic laugh. "No, no, no. I am is God, lovely. I am is simply that He is. There is nothing that's impossible because every time you say that word, you are, in fact, saying I'm-possible." The young Zion still didn't understand. "Every time that you feel alone, know that I am with you. It's okay to be scared, sad, angry, disappointed. But remember that He will never leave you, lovely."

* * * * * * * * *

"I am," Zion whispers into the wind, and it carries around her like a song. For a moment, she doesn't know how to feel. She still feels sadness, but it's like she is being comforted in a blanket of peace in her heart that she can't explain. She still feels like what happened to Chase was her fault, and she's being attacked on all sides, but it's like more arms are helping to hold the weight of it. It only makes her stronger. "I am not alone," she giggles like she just found out a secret.

"I'm not alone!" she repeats louder.

"Nope. But, there's no need to yell about it." Her head snaps to the side to find Jonathan seated with his head tilted like he is trying to solve a puzzle. "Why'd you run all the way here anyways, Flash? You could be dead, and no one would even know about it."

Zion blushes, "Why did you follow me if it was so dumb?"

He shrugs, "Your boyfriend and my girlfriend wouldn't stop whining about someone coming after you."

Zion rolls her eyes. "She's not your girlfriend."

"So, he *is* your boyfriend?" he wags his eyebrows suggestively, "I always knew you'd like the self-sacrificing type."

Zion feels more heat beneath her chocolate cheek bones. "You suck"

"Aren't teachers supposed to have advanced language skills or something?"

"I teach third grade!"

"I hope their vocabulary is better."

"Ugh! What. Do. You. Want?"

He looks like he ages before her eyes. "To live. Not just to survive, but to live free and unafraid for tomorrow." Both of them know that that isn't what she was asking, but it answers so much. "We live in dark times, Flash."

"Darkness cannot drive out darkness. Only light can do that."

"All right, Dr. King. Where do we get light from? Huh? When the darkness has swallowed it all up? Where does it come from?"

"We *become* the light, Jonathan. The dark can only win if we let our lights distinguish." Zion breathes deep and plunges on. "I'm new to this, but God has given us the power to overcome evil. We *can* live free."

"God left me a long time ago." Zion looks to the sky and thinks about the peace that she still feels in her bones. She remembers her grandmother and even Kateri, and she looks over at

Jonathan, who looks back with curiosity in his eyes. The wind picks up.

"Close your eyes..."

Chapter 26

ℒou want to do what!"

"A little louder next time, babe; your screeching can be a bit better." Adria cuts her eyes to Johnathan, who is dramatically rubbing his ears and he winks at her.

"I'm sorry if I'm the only one who's been in prison for a week." Adri defends, "I'm not in a hurry to go back."

"You weren't the only one," Khamira interjects from her place beside her mom. LaQuinn Noble has had a shadow everywhere she's gone since last night. And now a defender.

"Sorry," Adria grimaces at the other prisoner's treatment in the camp, "but if we want to live, we need to stay off the radar and not announce our presence with a blow horn."

"This is a matter of saving multiple people's lives. Think of every parent who accepted the *change* for fear of losing money or having no food. Some people thought that getting the mark of *change* was the lesser of two evils." Ravi says.

"And we can help them." Michael says, "Let's hear Quinn out."

Everyone has squeezed into the small room to discuss the next steps except for Aoife and Chaz, who apparently do not care and have struck up an unlikely friendship. Probably because Chaz likes to hear herself speak, and Aoife hardly speaks at all.

"We would have to go to a conference which is in a secure location to place a virus into the computer which regulates the *change* everywhere. They're going to the newly built temple in Israel."

"I can't be the only one who thinks that this is crazy. Zy?" Zion flinches when Adria says her name. She has been listening from her space on the floor, playing three-cup Molly with David.

"Well, I do think it's crazy—" Many voices shout in disagreement or consent, "—but. But!" She yells to get their attention once more, "We have to try. Suppose we can help more people around the world. It would be wrong for us not to."

"All right then!" Jonathan claps. "Majority rules, sorry babe, we're going to the conference."

"To get ourselves killed," Adria adds.

"Even if we die trying, our lives won't be in vain," Michael says, and everyone has varying responses to the cliché saying.

"And besides, now that big genius is here, there's no chance of error. No offense, smaller genius."

"Still offended." Khamira deadpans at Johnathan.

"I am glad that we have all come to a decision. Samael is taking the computer to Israel as we speak. Once all the leaders are together, we will be too late."

Like mother, like daughter. As always, very encouraging.

"So, how do we get to Israel?"

****

Buzzing. It's one of the most irritating sounds he hears all day because that means someone wants your attention. He'd much rather continue to sit back at his desk at headquarters. This is the first day in the office that he has had in weeks. But, of course, that won't last.

So, what's it going to be now?

He walks casually through the throng of people until he reaches an isolated spot that is usually reserved for the earth smokers.

Since he was supposed to accept the *change*, his HEDY should not be accepting contact. There's only one person that he knows who can bypass that security.

He gives his surroundings one more scan before answering.

"You survived," he says in lieu of hello as he slides a thin attachment behind his ear, and it latches to the skin with a tickle.

"It was only polite as I wouldn't want your efforts to have been wasted." He hears LaQuinn respond and smiles.

"It's good that you're okay."

"... For now." At that, Paul takes out a strip of gum. He knows he will need it.

"Somehow, I don't think this is a social call."

"I wish it were, but I do need your help. It'll be dangerous."

"I'm listening."

"Good. Are you near a computer?"

"Nope. The AI system EYES does most of the tech here. The few humans that we have are sentries. We just stand around and look pretty."

"Use your *vistegeum*." Quinn directs.

"Negative. It'll be picked up in less than a minute."

"We have it under control." Another voice joins. Younger. "If my mother and I didn't know what we were doing, then you'd already be dead."

"Enough," LaQuinn says fondly to what he assumes is her daughter before her attention is once again turned to him. "You'll be fine."

"For now." he parrots her words back.

"I'm going to set off some alarms as a distraction, but I need you to input this interference sequence into your HEDY. It will trigger your *vistegeum* into causing an error message in the main tracking system."

"Will anyone know that it was activated here?"

There is a pause. "It's likely."

This is where she gets me killed.

"What's the sequence?" He thinks *I may as well have some say in how I go. It's inevitable, anyway.*

She recites a series of letters and numbers in the phonetic alphabet, and Paul automatically remembers without instruction from years of training.

"As soon as you hear the alarm, put the sequence into your phone as if you're sending a transmission, then take the chip from the inside and input it into the drive nearest to you. You'll have 15 seconds."

"Roger."

"Are you ready?"

"I guess you can say that." She chuckles.

Woo! Woo!

Here goes. He quickly enters the code and then stands with his hand on his weapon, as does everyone else in the room. What he is actually doing is taking the chip out of his HEDY device.

"What's happening!" He yells to the room in general, noting the few members here and there. However, he is the highest-ranking officer, thankfully, so no one would suspect him being connected to this treason.

Ten seconds left.

"Sir— sir, an unauthorized flying apparatus was detected on radar in the southeast sector." A nervous-looking man answers.

"And?" *Hurry up.*

"The signal jammed. We've lost our communications, and the air apparatus looks like it's jumping into random points instead of flying straight. We can't track it."

"It could be terrorists!" A panicked lady adds shifting her weapon right and left as if someone will jump out at her at any moment. He fights not to roll his eyes.

"We will not take another loss! Find answers now! Search the perimeter!" He orders. He only has two to three seconds left. He quickly goes to the computer drive and adds the chip to it, lamenting the morons that he is surrounded by.

"Nice job." he hears in his ear.

"Was that 15 seconds?"

"No." His head drops, not liking failing. "But you had 20. Thank you. You really put yourself at risk."

He takes out a stick of gum. "All in a day's work, where are you headed?"

"Do you really want to know?"

"Loaded question."

"Israel."

Of course. "That's a pretty popular place to be these days. It might be crowded with celebrities and all."

"Live shows are always better," LaQuinn responds.

They end the transmission, and he gets up to assess the damage but comes face to face with his young protégé. He has kept Gabe close since their meeting with the General.

"Captain?"

Today is the day that the two of them were supposed to accept The *Change*. But this kid is the one person he has left to save. His mind steels, and he grabs his shoulder and leads him away. "It's about time we had a talk." He turns on his heel and thinks of favors that he is owed. "How do you feel about a vacation?" he mumbles with thoughts of a once Holy Land, "I just can't promise it'll be stress-free."

****

"The computer is in there?" David asks his brother.

"Yes," Ravi says, looking at a Colosseum, which leads to a hundred-foot-tall, rectangle-shaped temple, from which they are only able to see the top from their vantage point.

They can also see the vestibule, which Zion learned is a fancy word for porch, in front of an opening leading into an arched doorway that is large enough to fit a semi-truck. The brick and marble are lined with gold designs, and even the fence is white with gold trim, which makes the structure look like it is wearing an elaborate crown.

Every part of it looks purposeful and beautiful, and it's sad that they came here to do anything but show honor.

"You know, Davie, as impressive as this temple is, two others more immaculate have been brought down before." Ravi captures the young boy's attention.

"It looks like they fixed whatever was broken. I don't think it's coming down this time," he says.

Zion can't help but agree with him.

"Kid, you'd be surprised how effective subterfuge can be; the obvious attack is not always the best."

"Unless you've got the firepower," Chaz adds, walking into the room.

"Ah… And you always have the firepower, Charlotte."

"You know it," she responds with a badly veiled innuendo completed with a wink. Ravi smirks and reaches for her to come to him.

"Oh no!" David covers his eyes, "You guys are going to be gross!" He runs out of the room and Zion follows with a laugh, giving the couple a moment as well. *Who knows when they'll get another one?*

She approaches Michael, who is the only person taking his reprieve alone. He hears her approaching.

She settles near him, close enough that she is there if he wants to talk, but not trying to impose on his space. "Do you ever feel like it's too much? What if we can't do it?"

"For every beginning, there must be an end." He repeats his mother's last words to her.

"*Is* this the end?"

"What do you think?" He asks instead of responding. He is standing looking out of the window at the same building the others spoke about.

"A beautiful piece of architecture. The temple."

He looks at her and then back to the building.

"It is beautiful. I've seen models and read the descriptions and details, but I never imagined something so breathtaking. When I see this, it makes me sad. No. That doesn't even seem like enough of a word to describe it. This was a place for the Spirit of God to dwell." He exhales deeply. "But was this Holy place inspired by God or men?"

Zion looks over it, and she can see how a deity would reside here. It reminds her of the temples in Greece, which have statues of beautiful figures throughout, wrought with symbolism and history.

"Why would The Spirit need to stay inside?" She asks. "That kind of defeats the purpose of God, right?"

"How much time do you have?" He looks at her out of the corner of her eye, and she sees his eyes sparkle at the prospect of explaining to her.

"Give me the Cliff Notes version."

"What, no bedtime story?" She smiles and shakes her head at his joking. "Do you know Adam and Eve? They were physically there with God." He grabs her hand. "Close enough to touch."

That's distracting. She shakes her head and refocuses.

"The Ark of the Covenant was a way for God's presence to stay here with His people because of the sin of the world. They created a sacred place. This is where God's people would be able to communicate with Him, and the problem was that the people weren't perfect. There were so many steps that had to be taken to be worthy enough to get into the temple, and only a select few were able to go inside the Holy of Holies."

"But what happened? Did it get easier?" Zion has learned a lot about God and can now say that she believes in Him, but she wouldn't want to follow such a strict doctrine.

"Jesus."

"Jesus?" No one says that name anymore. People are even skeptical of naming their children in that fashion. You'll hear people occasionally, say spiritual, God, universe, or something, but never the name of Jesus.

"Yes, when He died, it made it so that we are all clean. Such a perfect sacrifice that we don't need to keep doing a lot to speak with God or to go to heaven."

"It's not... Why are people bad if he makes everyone clean? I mean, look at where we are. This place is being ruined by people. His sacrifice doesn't mean anything now. Everything good that we have has been taken from us!"

"You have to accept it, darling. But the opportunity is yours if you want it." And it suddenly doesn't feel like they are talking about the bad people anymore.

She is risking her life for the people, but looking at Michael's hazel eyes and holding his hand, it's like he is pleading for her to make a decision. Like this moment is going to change something inside of her.

"It sounds too good to be true. Like a fairytale," she whispers. "If I believe that I can be saved, I'll give power to it. And if it is not true, then I'll be lost."

He keeps looking into her eyes and waits in silence like he doesn't want to push, but she *needs* more.

And like her plea is answered, memories come back to her...

I am not alone.

Close your eyes...

He's alive!

Even if you close your eyes, I am still here.

I am. I am with you.

If you truly have an open heart, you will know the truth

Our imperfections make us who we are, but He loves us anyway. See, the thing is, plans only fail when it's in your power. Even when things look bad, God has something better than you can imagine for you. It doesn't mean that it's easy or what we call perfect, but you'll always come out a winner.

Zion has a strong surge of confidence. More than she has had with anything else. She doesn't want to fight with herself anymore. Cycling between doubt, desperation, and belief. Not when it's obvious.

There is no "your truth or my truth." There is only one Truth who is the way to life.

She smiles and opens her eyes to a mirrored smile before her. But there is something in his eyes that she can't quite name. She wants to explain it to him, but words aren't enough.

"I... I don't feel worried." She whispers. "It's like I'm... free?" Michael laughs and embraces her. "I am free!"

He picks her up and spins while they both laugh. It's completely

crazy, considering what they are doing here. Reality doesn't let them celebrate too long. Or rather, siblings don't.

"Well, well, well, this is an interesting development." Zion rolls her eyes at the Cheshire grin on Adria's face. "We *were* going to discuss this death trap plan again, but I'd understand if you didn't want to join." She says, wiggling her eyebrows.

"I should've left you in prison." Zion murmurs, and Michael laughs and squeezes her hand one more time before he turns and leaves the area to join the others. As soon as he leaves, she turns to her sister.

"Do you have to be yourself?"

"It's no fun being anyone else," she shrugs. "So...?"

"So what?"

"Is there something stirring? A romance, maybe?"

"Hello! You may have missed it, but there is a whole battle going on. The end of the world is here and all. No one has time for a relationship."

"I do." She says excitedly.

"You're not worried?"

"Nope. Johnathan is here—"

"He's 80% out of his mind."

"—And I have you, so what's there to worry about?"

"We could die." Zion deadpans.

"Well, I agree with what I heard and saw from you and lover boy. We'll be together no matter what happens."

Zion squints her eyes, "You know!"

"Of course, sis. I know everything." The two of them laugh at the age-old joke. "But seriously, I have had a lot of eye-opening experiences the last few days."

"That's wonderful!"

Adria opens her mouth to respond—

"Absolutely not!"

They hear raised voices from the other room, and both of their heads are angled to listen to what else is said.

"I guess that's our cue," Adria says, always eager to be in the middle of business that's not hers.

"Let's join the chaos, shall we."

Surprisingly, it turns out that it was Noble who was yelling.

"I am your mother whether you want me to be or not, and I am not going to say it again. You are staying here. I'm not losing another daughter to this war."

"You didn't lose her, you pushed her away! And now you're doing the same thing to me! You need me!" The teen's eyes are filled with tears that don't spill over.

"Khamira Anise. This conversation is over."

Said girl inhales deeply, and Zion is afraid that she will yell back, but she turns on her heel and stalks away.

LaQuinn looks like she wants to follow but decides against it. She sits roughly, putting her head in her hands, and speaks. "You may continue, Ravi."

Walking further, the women can see a crude drawing on the floor, which looks like a small rectangle inside of a larger one beneath a circle with a line across the diameter.

"We will enter here—" at the bottom of the larger rectangle— "then if we go quickly, we can cross the vestibule into the main chamber. This is most likely where the leaders will be convening. First, we will need a distraction and then a team to place the virus. I would like to volunteer for the latter."

"Okay. I'll ask." Johnathan joins, "What if the computer isn't there? Then the world is enslaved forever, and we die."

"We'll probably all be killed either way," Chaz adds helpfully.

"I am sure that it is here. The peace treaty with Israel will be signed here, and all of the world leaders are in one place for the rebuilt temple." LaQuinn informs them. "It's too big an opportunity for the leaders to pass up. Remember, I worked with them for years. This is where they will initiate the *change*, and then it will be too late."

"I should go with the big guy to place the virus since I am the best with people." Johnathan flashes a smile.

"No. I think that I should place the virus. I doubt it will be as easy as placing a chip. And I can locate the computer remotely. We only have one shot at this, so we must make it count."

"Well said, larger genius!"

"All right, now that the serious talk is done. We'll rush in and draw the attention of everyone while you place the virus." Chaz says, bouncing in excitement.

****

In retrospect, the small group should have known this couldn't be as easy as they hoped. But hindsight is 20/20.

"Ah!"

The group jumps and turns quickly to assess the threat.

Too late.

"Dead."

"What? We're all still alive." A quick look around confirms that Chaz is right.

"That's because I didn't want to kill you, but I have had the chance to kill each of you at least twice. The cocky one four times, but I really don't like him." A voice continues from the shadows, pointing out a pouting Johnathan.

Paul steps out of the shadows along with the soldier whom Michael shot with a dart. That seems like it happened so long ago when it has only been a week.

Both appear unbothered by the weapons pointed toward them, but the twitching in the younger man's hands gives him away.

"There's a kid here somewhere, right? He must have devised this plan to run right into the enemy's hand. It is cute, but let's leave the planning to the adults, shall we."

Zion's lips quirks upward, but everyone else doesn't seem to share in her amusement. Chaz, Oji, Aoife, and Johnathan have not dropped their weapons, and Michael has his in hand, assessing if friends or foes have discovered them.

"You should know better than to surprise war-hardened men and women." Oji comments in his accented voice, and Paul shrugs.

"With all the noise, I thought you all wanted company." The young counterpart adds and then looks away when all eyes shift to him.

Johnathan seems to be getting more agitated, and Adria, not one to sit still, walks in front of him with his arms crossed. "Stop it.

This one is my friend. And if he vouches for that other guy, then he's cool."

"It is true." Noble confirms, "They are no threat."

No one budges, and Adria finally exclaims, "If he wanted us dead, then we would be! We're wasting time with this."

Everyone's weapons drop, but Johnathan walks up to Adria and sidesteps with a wink at her and hardening when facing off with Paul.

"We meet again."

"Johnathan," Adria places her hand on his arm.

"You know, if you keep defending him, I may feel the urge to get rid of the competition."

"You're not this person anymore." She places her hand on his outstretched weapon.

He rolls his eyes and reluctantly walks away, pulling his love away from his current ire.

Zion exhales, *'That's one fight avoided'.* "What are you doing here?"

"And how did you find us?" Michael adds.

"Easy," Paul responds. "I kept the serial number. I took the liberty of looking around and got rid of some problems you would have encountered soon. Good thing I did, too, since none of you can survive without me. And the kid—"

"I'm Gabriel. You guys can call me Gabe since I'm joining your rebel group to take on the government." Everyone is silent, and he smiles awkwardly. "Nice to meet you."

Chaz bursts into laughter and slaps him on the back, clearing the awkward tension. "Glad to have you! Now, let's see what you two've got."

As corny and awkward as Gabriel is, he is great with a plan. He and Paul were completely in their element, making this work with most of them having basically no experience in this sort of thing.

First, Gabe, Jonathan, and Chaz will go through the vestibule (porch) to the main hall's doors. They will be posted around what should be the conference room to cause a distraction and hopefully get the computer isolated so that the core can disrupt the *change*.

Aoife and Oji both volunteer to get to the second story of the building to scout and provide cover if needed.

Michael and Adria will be next to enter from the other side of the room to get their hands on the computer. They are also supposed to look for another way out. No one knows exactly what to expect when they get in. The backup plan is for the two of them to take the core and computer back to Khamira to enable it.

Ravi and Noble will follow after. These two have the most important job. Obviously, when the opposition finds out what they are doing there, they will most likely be attacked. They will enter opposite Adria and Michael but have the advantage of being able to enable the core as soon as they get their hands on the computer.

Finally, Paul and Zion will come up the rear. To provide cover and keep the way out clear. It was Gabriel's idea to have him in the front and Paul in the rear since they could adjust the plan if needed.

They all wear HEDY devices, but Noble is sure that once The Alliance knows that they are there, they will disable them from each other. Throughout the temple there are uncovered spaces in the ceilings, so if worse comes to worse, they can climb the walls and get out of there.

"All right, fledglings, let's move out," Paul says. "We don't want to keep our guests waiting."

The closer the group gets, the more Zion wants to go back. But back to where? She doesn't know, but she is fighting every instinct that she has with every step. She tries to encourage herself but can't get out of her mind.

This is a good plan.

"No, it's not," Paul responds. Did she say that out loud? "But it's the only plan that we've got. So, keep your head up, 'right?"

She takes a deep breath and waits until they can see LaQuinn and Ravi descend into the valley. She sees Paul move, ready to enter the vestibule, but her body doesn't respond. She feels her breath coming way too fast, and her chest tightens. She's spiraling. She is headed straight into a panic. The blood is pounding into her ears.

"I can't..." She whispers. She knows that no one can hear it, but she doesn't stop. "I can't, I can't," she repeats several times until she's just mouthing the words with no sound coming out.

"Hey." Her partner roughly grabs her arms and shakes her. If she wakes up tomorrow, she's sure that her neck will be sore, "We don't have time for this, so shake it off."

"I don't —— I'm not this person I have to go back I have to – I need to—"

He shakes her again. "Cut it out!"

Their eyes meet, and she feels her's watering. Paul's gray orbs roll in exasperation, "Listen, girl, none of us actually have the power to do anything, and it's presumptuous for you to think *you,* of all people, make any difference. Don't you dare cry! Do you hear me? Don't be afraid of death. Don't be afraid of any man. Fear is not in you." He pokes her in the chest. "Have faith and remember we're in this together. All of us."

Zion grabs his hand and nods with deep breaths. She focuses on his steadiness. She notices him taking dramatic, slow inhales and exhales, and she mimics it until the two of them are matching.

"Good, you're ready?"

"Yes. Thanks."

"Great." Zion jumps at the sudden voice in her ear. *"Because if you don't get going, you're going to ruin everything."*

"Kami?"

"Yeah. Just because I'm not coming in, doesn't mean I'm not coming with you."

Somehow, that makes her feel even better. "Let's go."

* * * * * * * * *

The first 10 minutes went by without a hitch. The only person she has seen since coming in is Paul, who is now at the other end of the room, having gone ahead to secure the area.

Was it crazy to believe that everything would be a stress-free success?

Zion is unsure of exactly what caused it, but she doesn't have the time to think about it as she turns her face over her shoulder and notes how close the faceless shadow guards chasing her are.

Her steps pound on the smooth pavement. If not for the thunderous herd of footsteps behind her, she would feel quite small and such a huge place.

"Ah!"

She just barely turns a corner in time to miss a very real bullet that takes the place where her head was moments before. The high privacy hedges that she scoffed at before are so much more appealing while she is trying to outrun the shadow guards of Hades.

If only she could just reach Paul. Why did she think that it was a good idea for him to go ahead without her? She is no challenge to these people, and he's the one with the plan, right?

She hears Kami's voice urging her on, but it's nothing compared to when she hears his.

"Let's go! Let's go! Let's go!" She hears him before she sees him urging her to the doorway he has kept open. She pushes herself to go faster until she reaches him, not even slowing when she finally gets through the door.

"They're —— they're close." She pants from her space near the wall she almost ran into.

"This may be a spot of trouble."

"You think!" Zion turns toward him just in time to see Paul toss a hand grenade into the room she just exited and closes the door hard.

Boom!

"Oh." she exhales.

"Don't relax yet. That will only slow them down, and we need to find the brains of this operation."

"That optimism must be why you have so many friends," she mumbles sarcastically, following him.

"This is my thanks for saving you?" He chuckles, keeping his eyes moving along every surface. "We need to catch up to the others. I doubt that these are only guests."

Zion only nods and speeds up so that she isn't left behind again. She keeps her breath even, though she wants to groan with the pain from the stitch in her left side, and her muscles have been sore for the past few days.

Paul's critical eyes glance back at her, and she doubts he misses it, but he doesn't say anything and definitely doesn't slow down.

She follows him through the temple. She is once again floored by the designs in the anti-chamber that they enter. One wall is almost entirely a window, but the edging makes it like a diamond, which reflects light from the ten strategically placed lanterns outside it. It makes it seem as if you are walking into a star.

The room has four large square pools in each corner. And high ceilings make the room feel larger. There is a wall opposite the window which has a marble overlay with bronze trim and gold specs throughout, which wink and twinkle with each step she takes. There are ten bronze bowls in the shape of hands cupped together, each with some type of powder or liquid, standing on pure white podiums.

As much as Zion wants to take in every detail of the room — even the floor has six-pointed stars etched onto each tile, which can be mistaken for texture if one is not paying attention to it. The scholar in her wants to search every piece of the puzzle in this place and figure out the significance of it all. But the pair are getting closer to raised voices.

They face bronze double doors with angels on the front. Their wings cover their faces and come together, making handles.

On opening them, Ravi and LaQuinn are peeking through a hole with grim faces. They can hear the voices of what she now sees are the leaders speaking over one another in what must be the main hall. Each of the group peers into the hall through small, steeple-shaped holes in the wall.

"We're too late," Ravi says. "We need to retreat."

"Retreat to what?" Noble says with little patience. "All of those people who died... we can't turn back now."

"Everyone knows! The whole world has had its chances to not conform to this monster. They've heard the Scriptures! They know the prophecies!" Zion glances into the room to ensure no one hears Ravi's raised voice. "We can't *make* anyone do anything. Why is it our job to save these people who would not think twice about letting us get tortured and killed?"

"Well, you two? Do you agree? Should we hide and hope for another day of not being discovered? Should we value our lives above everyone else's?"

Zion cringes at being brought into the argument. "We can't choose whether we live or die, but we can choose what we do with our lives. I... I say we try."

"Well said," Paul says from his space near the wall, not taking his eyes off his targets in the main hall. He doesn't turn, but the occupants feel his attention shift to the taller man. "Don't think for a moment that the people in that room don't know we're here. There's no backing out now. Tough luck, you've got to be a hero."

Ravi doesn't look happy. In fact, this is the most frustrated that Zion has seen him, but he doesn't respond (as painful as that looks to be).

"There's a case near the seat in the center of the room if my calculations are correct — and they are — that's what you need to reach."

Zion tips her toes and sees that the case she mentioned is a significant distance from them and surrounded by people. "How do we get in? We already ran into guards earlier." Which reminds her that it has been a while since they have heard anything. What's going on?

"From what I have seen, this antechamber circles the entire room, but there are only actually two ways in and one upstairs.

Oji and Aoife are already headed up, and everyone else is finding the best positions." LaQuinn answers.

"I'm opening the channel," Khamira says. *"Guys. You all have each corner of the room covered, but there are only two doors to enter the main room. The guards have stopped for some reason, but there are a lot of them just outside of the room where you are. That's not good."*

"The guards were given specific instructions not to enter the room unless there is a sure threat. They most likely have alerted the leaders of our presence, but they won't make a move until we show ourselves. They aren't high enough up on the food chain to hear what's being said and done." Noble clarifies.

"I'm insulted that they don't see us as a threat," Johnathan adds.

"Johnathan, Chaz, and what's his name? It will take time to get in the room, so be careful because the guards will probably come in to kill quickly." Khamira ignores him.

"I'll take down the back entrance when we get through," Gabriel says.

"This is a suicide mission." Ravi finally chips in.

"We need that computer," Paul responds firmly. "We'll create a distraction. You just do your part."

LaQuinn takes out the core, and Zion sees the same ethereal blue disk that she was given by Kateri the last time she saw her.

"Where did you…?" Zion trails off.

"My intelligent daughter took it off your hands the first day you came to the bridge. Even then, things were working for us. We will do this."

"Anything else you want to say to your kid?" Paul asks her with his comm device in his hands. They all hear what he doesn't say. The chances are that they won't all make it out alive.

"I have said what I need to to each of my children. I… I need time to get the device."

He nods, not touching on her choice. Sometimes, not saying goodbye is easier.

"We'll make sure you have time to plant it." Paul begins to pull out grenades and guns. He thrusts something into Zion's hands. She looks down at her single handheld weapon and compares to the heavily armed man beside her.

"I feel underdressed."

He rolls his eyes and passes one to the others, which they take with much more confidence than she did.

No need to overwhelm myself. She reminds herself.

"Ready?" She nods.

"Be careful." He nods back, and her lips lift. "I wish we were on the same team longer."

"We'll make a soldier out of you yet, little bird." He pulls her goggles onto her face to her confusion. "Close your eyes!" He says loudly to everyone.

"Why ––"

"Now!"

Flash!

Chapter 29

Move!"

And like a slingshot being released, everyone bounds forward into the main hall.

The flash bomb did its job, and most of those in the room are scrambling and yelling over each other, now in a panic.

Ten seconds after the flash bomb goes off, another joins with more damage and much more noise.

Zion crouches down, instinct to cover her neck and head, but from her new vantage point, she sees... the case!

She runs toward it, grabs the handle, and turns in circles frantically trying to find LaQuinn.

"Zion... top of the case... get out... Zion!" Khamira is saying something to her, but their signal is all but gone, and with all of the chaos around her, she can't understand.

"Kami, I can't— Ah!" she screams.

Her hair is caught in a death grip— this is no time for puns— and she's face-to-face with... A beast.

How can she describe him in any other way? She has seen him on screens multiple times, but the camera doesn't catch the glint in his eyes or his animalistic snarl.

He smiles triumphantly down at her and quickly looks around to see many of the leaders running while the guards are entering the room and being held off by the Adherens and their Allies. He drags her by her hair and she brings with her the case with the much-desired computer.

She continues screaming and tries to pull and punch at him to make him let go.

He swings her back against the wall, and she is frozen in a silent scream of shock and pain.

He brings his face mere inches away from hers. His manicured hand gently caresses her face, the antithesis of the brutal hand holding her in place.

"Of course, you're here." His voice is gentle like he's speaking to a frightened child. Zion stiffens as he comes closer, pressing his nose into her hair, and breathing deeply, taking in her scent. His proximity makes it so that she does the same dispute her resistance, and her senses are taken over by spice. The smell burns her throat as it travels to her lungs.

She wishes he stunk and that his hands were rough. He should look like the evil that he is. The worst type of monster is the one who doesn't look like one.

"Zion." He hisses like the snake that he is. "I will have great pleasure from your death."

She remains silent only because she doesn't want to agree with him. Is it possible to kill what's already damned?

"Zion." She fights not to jump at Khamira in her ear. *"I don't have much time. They are already trying to lock me out. To your right. Get the core and get out!"*

She turns her head away from him and sees LaQuinn looking pointedly at the suitcase, which is still tight in her grip. His gentle hand goes to grab her neck in a painful hold.

"Behold, I lay in Zion a choice stone, a precious cornerstone. And whoever believes in Him will not be disappointed." He lets out a manic laugh. "Your death will be the end of the rebellion. Everyone will see my truth. This world is mine."

Her fingers inch to her weapon. "I... think...not!"

Pew!

Abigor shrinks back with a roar, and Zion tosses the suitcase back to LaQuinn's waiting hands. She scrambles back but doesn't get far before a kick to the ankle brings her down, another follows to her ribs.

She is close enough to the main room to hear the sounds of shouting and shooting. She crawls towards it, knowing that it's safer in the chaos there than the alternative of staying here with him.

"It's fitting." She hears him following leisurely, but his voice is strained. "You—a woman— now crawling on your belly away from me! Oh, how the tables have turned."

She resists the urge to look at him. He allows her to enter into the great room, and the advantage that they had from surprise is now gone. She looks around, and her heart drops.

Gabriel, Michael, Chaz, Paul, and Jonathan are in the middle of the room back-to-back, facing opponents on every side. Oji looks critically injured, maybe dead. Aoife is shooting guards down from up above. She doesn't see Adria, but that only gives her more anxiety.

Even with limiting the enemy from coming in on multiple sides, they are getting overwhelmed. They are tired and don't have unlimited ammunition.

"You will all die one by one." Zion doesn't look back or reply, but she pushes to her knees and then to her feet, and he allows it with a chuckle.

I refuse to die lying on the ground like a coward.

She looks up at the sky, wondering if she will soon see beyond. *I hope I see you, God, and that you're pleased. I hope we win, and please, if any miracles are left. Help my friends. They deserve life. They deserve freedom.*

She hears the small click, and she holds her breath.

"No!"

She whips around to see wild, curly hair, pressing a hand against Abigor's neck.

"Adria!"

The General Elect stumbles back, and her savior appears to not have been unarmed. There is now a small knife handle sticking dangerously close to his neck. He growls in pain, and both ladies reach for each other.

"Watch out!"

The two turn to see Jonathan pointing a large gun toward them. A look behind them reveals their General taking out a gun at the same time.

Two shots ring out, and they jump backward as the ceiling collapses, making a barrier between them and their most dangerous adversary.

Zion looks at the barrier and realizes that Johnathan protected them.

"I hope he's dead. Is that... wrong?" Adria pants.

"No, it's not." Zion chuckles, turning toward her sister. "I'm just glad we got away before he ——" It would seem that the General Elect did not miss.

Chapter 30

"No, no no no no no no no no no."

Blood is supposed to be thicker than water, but somehow, it still seeps between each crease of Zion's hands as she tries to stem the flow from her sister's chest.

"Zy...Zion." Adria coughs.

"I'm here."

"We really... Kicked his butt. I... Told you. I never... Lose a fight..." Adria coughs red, staining her lips.

"The fact that you got away has to count for something," Zion says, reminded of Adria coming home after a bad fight with her abusive boyfriend when she said the same words.

"I..." Adria rasps. Zion can barely feel her pulse, and she feels so cool, "I'm not scared... But... Will you... Stay?"

Zion choked on the sob. She keeps her hand on her chest, ignoring the blood and counting each beat of her weakening heart.

"Even if you close your eyes. I'll be here."

Adria smiles and gasps as she places her hand on top of Zion, and her chest falls.

It doesn't rise again.

****

Zion hears but doesn't hear. She sees but doesn't see. Her body is betraying her by breathing when she feels dead. She still holds her hand to her sister's heart, waiting for a beat.

"What are you doing?"

I don't care. She doesn't respond verbally, and she can't be bothered to.

"Stop! We can end this!" There is a response, but Zion is waiting patiently for Adria to move. If she turns away, she could miss it.

"You have no idea ––" a different voice. Male this time, "–– we can't interrupt the prophecy. These things have to happen!"

Zion blinks, confused. It's registering that they aren't speaking to her. But what are they talking about?

"Prophecy? You can't decide what will make it come to pass. If it is time, it will happen, but if we have the ability, we must help others. We must!"

That sounds like LaQuinn. And maybe Ravi. She didn't see him in the main hall. Zion knows that she should go and investigate, but... Adria looks happy with a small smirk like she knows a secret. There is no more blood flowing, and her eyes are glazed over. Zion kisses her on her forehead and shuts her lids, hiding her coffee eyes for the last time.

"Even if you close your eyes..." She promises.

She rises from the floor and turns away. She takes one step and then another and another, the load getting heavier with distance, never easing, but she keeps going. Step-by-step.

"...I'll be here."

The voices. That's her goal. Go to the voices. It looks like Jonathan's shot took down the ceiling and wall behind the anti-chamber, and Zion has a small view of the rest of the team who have taken shelter behind a similar barrier. It looks like they are moving toward her.

If they progress quickly, they can reach her in minutes. They've done a good job of keeping the guards from swarming them, but she knows that won't last.

Zion retraces her steps to where she threw the computer to LaQuinn, and …Her eyes flit back and forth, and she remembers the conversation between the two, piecing the puzzle together with what she sees. LaQuinn is holding the computer, and the core is dropped in front of her feet, but —

"Please don't do anything you will regret, Ravi."

Said man is holding his gun pointed toward the elder woman. "Oh, I won't regret it. Drop the computer and walk away." He commands.

"What will you do with it?"

"The famine, illness, wars, the river drying. It's all right here. I'm going to make sure it comes to pass."

"I love my children. I have to do this."

There is a lull; the two make eye contact, neither budging. Noble opens her mouth to respond, but the ground starts to shake, and the building sounds like it's falling around them. Ravi barely keeps his feet, and Noble sees her chance.

She dives for the drive and opens the screen. She jabs the core toward its destination and—

Pew!

Not fast enough.

Zion inhales sharply, unbelieving, and LaQuinn's hands fall away, and she falls limp.

"No!" Zion ducks just in time to avoid joining her as another shot skims by her.

He tried to shoot me. She isn't alone in her panic for long.

"Are you okay?" Michael asks her, looking at the blood on her hands. She doesn't answer because her mind is overfilled with emotions. "Zion?"

She shakes her head. "No... Adri—"

"I know. I'm so sorry, darling."

"Ravi! He tried to shoot me!"

"Paul and Chaz are following him. Quinn is— she's gone." He sighs and drags his hand along his face. "What were we thinking?"

"We were going to save the world." She says with a sad smile.

"I've never been so wrong." She frowns and places her hand behind his neck, tickling the tufts of hair there. "My mom was so sure, but I just... I don't believe it."

"We're on the winning team, remember? It's not over yet."

"We were wrong. About all of it."

Her brows furrow in confusion. "What are—"

"'Ey!" They turn to see Aoife rounding a corner and throwing a weapon behind her. "The company is arriving!"

Zion barely has time to marvel at all of the words that she said. Just behind Aoife, Jonathan is yelling like a madman and aiming his two guns this way and that. He looks terrifying, not only because he is covered in blood.

"The walls 'ave been taken down," Aoife says when she reaches them. "We've lost the cover. Will soon be surrounded and die."

It might've been better when she didn't speak.

"We have to catch up with the others. Maybe we can make it out of here."

Zion makes eye contact with Jonathan's anguished eyes.

"I…" She looks away, unable to face her mirrored emotions in another's eyes.

"No need to be alarmed." He says with false enthusiasm. "I'll buy you guys some time."

"No." She whispers.

"Are you crazy? You'll die!" Michael exclaims as Jonathan loads three handguns and a rifle, which appears to have been taken from a shadow guard. His hands pass over three small balls, which she knows are grenades of some sort.

"I'm way too much fun for you flower girls anyway." The stampede of footsteps gets closer. "I never planned on sticking around for long."

Aoife nods and begins to walk away. Michael shakes his head but eventually follows. Zion looks at his dark hair as he turns back to face his opponents and stands as a protector over his lover's body.

"You don't have to do this." She hears herself say. He doesn't face her but stays at the ready.

"I've lived free, and I'll die free."

I get it, Adri. Why you could never say goodbye.

Michael backtracks to pull her away.

Maybe we'll see each other again...

****

Tonight is going as well as Paul expected, which is not very. The only difference is that he thought they'd all be dead by now.

Partners unaccounted for, half of them are dead or incapacitated, comms have been disconnected, and one member has gone rogue. He sighs, just thinking of the mess that they have made.

He can guess what happened to Quinn, and his teeth grit, itching for some gum. He has no time to ask questions, but he intends to get answers.

Charlotte (it's Chaz!) has been mumbling under her breath since the two of them saw Ravi turn his gun on Zion. She went from shock to fury faster than he could blink. She shouted after him for a time before she turned her ire inward.

He should be worried about her conflict of interest but needs to finish the mission and get the case to Quinn's daughter.

"Stop," Paul says. "It's quiet." The sounds of fighting and shouts have ceased. Without words exchanged, the two of them stick to the walls and advance much slower.

They come to the corner and hear quiet shuffling of feat. They nod to each other, and weapons face off.

Aoife, Zion, Michael Paul, and Chaz come face-to-face. His eyes sweep the group, and he realizes another is missing. He never should have brought Gabe into this.

Everyone exhales, but anxiety is still high.

"Did you guys find Ravi?" Zion questions, stepping out from behind Michael. Paul sighs exasperatingly seeing her still unarmed. "He has the core. We can't have come here for nothing." She pauses, looking at Chaz, who Paul thinks is romantically involved with the traitor. "I'm sorry."

"What happened to you?" Chaz says instead of responding. "You weren't even fighting."

She is right. There young woman looks like an animal hunted for sport. She's holding her ribs, her hair has come loose, and she has blood all over her. He chooses not to comment and answers her question.

"He ran ahead. But the situation has changed. We lost sight of him, and… we should abort."

He sees grim faces and a fiery Asian. "We are not leaving! That rat! We'll get him first *and then* leave! I was betrayed!"

"Look at us, Chaz," Michael pleads, "we should regroup. We may get another opportunity if we leave now."

"This is our only opportunity."

Everyone pauses at Zion's words. They look at each other, and they all know it's true. Chances are they don't make it out of here anyway.

"All right. Remember, our objective is to find the case or Ravi. Preferably both. If you get the case, go to the kid and leave. Don't worry about anyone else."

"Let's get 'em before something gets us," Zion states with fake enthusiasm.

As if summoned, bright lights blind them in an assault. Paul sighs sharply and raises both his hands.

I could really use a stick of gum.

Chapter 31

They are surrounded. There is no way to leave now. Ravi led them straight into a trap. She'd say that it was on purpose, but the man is on his knees with three guns point-blank against his head. They are all being shepherded to his side.

Clap. Clap. Clap.

The slow clapping makes her look up into the smiling face of Samael Abigor. The General Elect is standing on a raised podium, looking pleased. There are two drones flying in circles around his head, slowly taking in the scene.

He smiles at the camera and lifts his one good arm. His injuries looked treated, but his clothes still scream of a beating. Like a wounded man returned from a battlefield, he is projecting the image of a war hero.

Zion looks at the drones flying above them, and she can just imagine the story. <u>Terrorists destroy the temple in a fit of rage. The nonconformists once again show their true colors.</u>

Looking at his freshly polished face contrasting their bloody, battered ones. She expects to feel heat burning at her bones or any strong emotion, but she just feels....

"Sorry for you."

Eyes face her from all around, though she spoke in barely a whisper. She holds her head high and speaks up. "I feel sorry for you. So consumed by hate and your desire to be God that you are missing out on true love. On true *life*! You claim that the Adherens are stuck in the past, clinging to a dead religion? But the truth is that you are the one stuck. You have no power, Samael. You will face eternity inferior to a being that you can only dream of emulating."

A sharp burn of pain hits the back of her popliteal, making her kneel. She glares defiantly through watery eyes at the shadow guard who attacked her.

"I will show all of The World Alliance that your God is a lie. Everything you stand for and everyone who stands with you is naught. Bring her."

Zion feels arms beneath her shoulders, roughly pulling her along, and she can barely get her feet underneath her to follow without being dragged.

"Stop! She doesn't know anything!" Michael is restrained, and one of the guards places a weapon on his head. "Bring her back!"

The General pauses and signals his man to stand down. "I will bring her back." Everyone pauses in confusion but he continues, "and you can grieve her body. And your defeat."

Michael's struggle increases tenfold and two guards manhandle him to the ground. But it is nothing compared to the damage being done to Paul. The guards seem to have a personal vendetta against him. Chaz and Aoife are putting up a fight against their assailants, though the former looks as if she is trying to get to Ravi, who just looks pained and resigned.

Abigor smirks and walks forward, and Zion is roughly forced to follow.

"All of the traitors will be dealt with, and then we will find every link to the chains of bondage and finally be victorious." She hears him murmuring quietly.

"Do you actually believe that?" Zion asks as they reach a tall archway.

It is beautiful and has curtains of purple and gold following the theme throughout the temple. It looks as if diamond is etched into the folds. The royal purple curtains are held back by angels on each side. They have six wings that join together to clasp the curtains closed. When the curtains open, there will be an angel on each side. As if to judge if you are worthy enough to enter.

"It doesn't matter if I believe it," he interrupts her admiration, "only that *they* do," he murmurs before continuing in a voice for the cameras to hear. "The Holy of Holies is said to be the most sacred place. A place where God himself dwells. If you were to enter this place, His wrath would overcome you, and you would die." He jabs a finger at her. "That is the power of your God. But I will show you power."

The General grabs Zion's wrists and yanks her even more forcefully than the two guards had and the pain in her ribs and knee intensifies, but she holds her tongue. *It won't be long now.*

When she reaches the door, she plants her feet. The stories of old may not mean anything to him, but Zion does not want to see God's wrath for invading His space.

Unfortunately, Abigor does not seem to care as he pulls her forward. She holds her breath as they cross the threshold. Nothing happens. Yet.

"Ha..." He is in disbelief as he looks right and left. He begins to laugh wildly and releases her wrist. How do the people not see his wickedness? Her adversary takes a deep breath and chuckles.

His blue eyes land on a chest made of gold with cherubim on the design. The Ark of the Covenant.

When he reaches it, he holds his arms above it, hesitating before he commits and grabs it firmly with both hands.

"I have looked upon the face of God and lived." He whispers. The three drones circle the room, getting every angle for the crowds. She can imagine the way that this film will be used in the future agenda.

"*My* people. Who are called by *my* name. Accept this freedom. No one will ever oppress you again. Follow *me*. Believe in *me*."

"You are a liar!" Zion can't hold back for one more moment. He stands in this place full of disrespect. "God is not some dead myth but the truth! A living being who reigns over heaven and earth, and everyone will bow to him, including you!"

Fury overtakes his face, but he doesn't lash out like she expects. Instead, he steps up to The Ark and uses it as a seat. No, a throne. It's a mockery, and he knows it.

"Everything your God can do, so can I! I create life. I decide justice. *My* will be done! I. Am. God!"

A chill overtakes the room and seeps into Zion's bones at his words. In contrast, a fire starts at her core, shifting over every inch of her skin, even to the strands of her hair.

The heat travels through her. Searching. It collides with the cool weight in her bones. The two temperatures battle within her, causing friction. She feels like she is exploding. Like every inch of her is being disintegrated.

But if that were true, wouldn't she hurt? She actually can't feel any pain. Even her collective injuries from the last few days, feel whole. The warmth is... unadulterated love. It's a first kiss, a mother's hug, a newborns laugh, a welcome home. Every good feeling she has ever felt converges inside of her. It grows until it is overwhelming.

Zion breathes and embraces it.

Is there ever a time when you look death in the eye and are not afraid?

Yes.

It's like time freezes. Like eternity and time have joined together.

Lightning strikes across the sky; word will spread of a space storm overtaking the skies. In the span of milliseconds, light waves travel across the banner of the sky in every part of the world. No corner is untouched.

But in a blink, it is over.

Samael Abigor, the General Elect of The World Alliance, looks in fear to the sky, but his penance doesn't immediately come. Finally, he exhales and turns with a smirk to his captive, only... She is gone. Vanished. His face is frozen as he walks over robotically and grabs the clothes that she wore.

He balls them up in his hands until his fist clinches. Only one drone remains, the others destroyed in the storm, and it is trained on him as he lets out a mighty roar toward heaven.

Time starts now.

There is not a person who does not see the spectacular light display in the sky, but it doesn't distract from the chaos that covers the land. Millions of people vanish from existence, and the video of one Zion Freeman vanishing before the General is frequently being analyzed as the start of the phenomenon.

Others show similar proof of people simply disappearing in the blink of an eye. No current technology can explain the event. Scientists have taken to saying that those who were affected by the event underwent The *Completion*. But still they have been unable to answer, will it happen again? Aliens, sickness, and many other explanations are given, but the truth is that the clock has started.

He came back.

****

The steps of the trio echo off of the walls. The entire space is empty, but of course it is. All of those within were followers of The Way. They truly believed.

"So what should we do?" The accent of his partner garners his attention. "We 'ave no resources. No men."

"I don't know. I don't know what to do…"

"Why did you not go with them?" Aoife asked.

"Because…" He starts, "I did not truly believe. I was against the government oppression, and everyone I loved was a part of the Adherens, a faithful group that refused to conform. It just made sense for me to quote what they did. What they were saying was so good… it was too good. I wanted to follow my family and stand for something. But when things weren't going the way thought that they should, I realized it was not real to me. Just a good story. I never truly believed it for myself. People who believe in something fight harder. I just wanted to win."

"But no more?" She asks him.

"No. No more."

"There must be others we can find. They will trust you."

"You're right. We have to try to reach as many as we can. We missed the first call, but it's not too late."

Aoife nods, "First, we find who else was left behind." She walks away into the Bridge, and when he goes to follow, he pauses in front of a mirror and faces himself.

I should've listened, Mother. Michael's hazel eyes show heartbreak and great sorrow. "I truly am sorry." He doesn't say who he is speaking to, but he hopes that he has the strength to keep going. The last hour has just begun. There is no time to waste.

To be continued…

ACKNOWLEDGMENTS

To my Lord and Savior, Thank You for giving me this dream and giving me the means to get it done. When I literally quit, it was you who told me to try again and keep going.

To my mother, who showed me how to be persistent and to follow my dreams. You have taught me how to hold on to Jesus Christ and let him guide me in everything I do. Thank you.

To my family, who have ALWAYS shown such support to me. I love you and thank you.

To my editing, creating, and publishing team. Thank you all for using your talents and making this possible

To the readers for supporting and encouraging me with love. Thank you

About the Author

Zipporah is a young woman who has been writing stories ever since she was very young. She remembers telling tall tales to her friends and family, and in the eighth grade, she won a young authors contest. She was introduced to fanfiction as a teenager and loved to see the alternate endings to some of her favorite shows and books. In her teenage years, she began to write to release all of the emotions that she couldn't understand or articulate in person. She began to feel freedom in her writings. She comes from a Christian family but developed a true relationship with Christ as a young adult in 2019. From this spiritual change, she began to see the world differently and saw many areas in the world that were messy and broken. She started volunteering for outreach and missions overseas.

Her passion is helping people to see themselves the way that God does and loving them through the life that they are living. The stories that she writes now are inspired by that dream.

Part 2

"What are you doing here?"

"I need your help."

"It's too late. They're already gone. It's too late." The woman is sitting in all white. Even the room that she is in is devoid of color. She rocks back and forth, and her neck makes jerking movements every so often. She looks ill. Unstable. But there is no one else.

"Please. I know that you helped with the *change*. There is no one else who can help us. You have to come with me."

"I can't. It's too dangerous." Her voice is going up in pitch. "Shut up." She abruptly faces a blank wall, staring intently as if there is more than meets the eye. "We can't do that." She continues to her hallucination.

He looks at her and begins walking slowly toward her, making sure to maintain eye contact. There is so much that he has found out about her. So much that she tried to do for all of them, and now this is what she has become.

He continues steadily until he reaches her, and she watches him approach, tensing more and more with each step. When he is a breath away, she stops rocking.

She stands with shaking hands and reaches for his face. He is perfectly still, knowing that she can spiral out of control at the slightest inconsistency.

Finally, she touches both sides of his face, and her eyes widen.

"You're real." He nods.

"Elisha... We need you to create a counter for the *change*."